# What If?

# What If?

**Written By:**
Valerie Hodge
Kelli A. Wilkins
Marian Powell
Ian Lamberto
Justin R Woolley
Dixie Sorensen
John J. Rust
Grace Gannon Rudolph
Paul A. Freeman
Stevie Poppe
Harper Hull
Derek Rutherford
Don Magin
Jennifer Caddell

Edited By Casey Quinn

ISBN: 978-0-9822434-3-5


Published by:
ReadMe Publishing
http://readme.us.com

# Table of Contents

# INTRODUCTION
## *By T. M. Hunter*

*What if?*

Two simple one-syllable words, rather bland and dull. Individually, either alone or stuffed into the middle of the rest of a sentence, they're usually ignored. Like extras in a movie scene, they may set up the surrounding milieu, but everyone watching has come to see the real stars of the show.

But when these two lightweights join forces, they become the major attraction. That's why this simple two-word question has become the focal point for all of the best speculative fiction.

The stories within this anthology were chosen for their ability to catch the reader by asking that very question. Each focuses on a different aspect of this world or another, and begs the reader to ponder, what if? Then, each story takes the leap forward, and leads everyone on a journey to discover the answer.

And that in itself is the biggest expectation out of any piece of speculative fiction.

So, sit back, kick your feet up, and enjoy this selection of stories. May it inspire you to continue asking yourself that most powerful question.

*What if?*


**About T.M. Hunter**

T. M. Hunter is an avid aircraft and space junkie when he finds those brief moments of free time between his day job and writing space opera novels and short stories. His first Aston West novel, Heroes Die Young, was honored as Champagne Books' Best-Selling Novel of the Year for 2008. He has had several short stories published with his Aston West story "Little White Truths" receiving a top-ten finish in the 2007 Preditors and Editors Readers Poll. His next Aston West novel, Friends in Deed, is scheduled for a January 2010 release. More information about his stories, novels and upcoming events can be found at AstonWest.com. He can also be followed at MySpace and Facebook (under the name Aston West) and Twitter (@astonwest).

# EXTRA GOOD CARE
## *By Valerie Hodge*

*There are certain things you must know about lying before you lie to a liar. Because more times than not, we find ourselves telling the truth in the form of a lie just to keep ourselves from feeling like a betrayal. Imagine a power, a certain defined ability, where lying becomes impossible. How would we survive? How would we justify some of the urges of our human nature? Because more times than not, we are a liar. And the only way that we discover this truth is through the vibe of a guilty conscious. A person who can look you in the face with a sort of compassion. Making you feel as though what you have done to them, will change the things. Forever.*

*More often than not this isn't the case. But then how can one single person make anyone feel anything that is as overwhelming as guilt? After all, isn't guilt supposed to be bigger than any of us?*

*This is how I began to believe that not everyone is human. Some of us believe in an afterlife, others in the supernatural, and others in the sheer sense of knowledge as power. But sometimes the simplest form of power comes through the words we speak. The things we can make people believe. The ways we are manipulated against our will. Against even our own recollection.*

*Because the one thing that we can all agree on in this world, is that not everyone is good inside.*

\*\*\*

When I was ten years old the only thing that I was truly good at was writing diary entries. I told anyone who would listen that I would someday become a famous author and therefore spent countless hours heaving my heart and soul into a 30 page coiled scribbler. Aside from an occasional poem that turned out okay, most of my other writing was crap. But the one type of writing that never failed to show my true colors, also happened to be my favorite hobby – writing in my diary.

Every Monday morning I would wake up, ready to embrace the weekly routine I would never learn to adapt to. Tuesdays and Thursdays were piano lessons, Wednesdays were for soccer practice, and Fridays were always "Dad Days". So as in many other ways, I was quite different than most of the kids my age; Instead of dreading Mondays, I actually learned to embrace them. Every other day of the week had some sort of poisonous, conspiracy-driven, conformatized, absolute and utterly hideous form of activity that I hated. I would sometimes lay in bed for hours after the gentle and also routine tuck-in by my mother, and try to devise some sort of plan to destroy the organized activities once and for all! There was the straight posture required by piano that I could never withhold, the lousy sport genes that just happened to run in my family, and of course the Dad who tried way too hard to impress his little girl when really, he knew nothing about her or anything she enjoyed. It just so happened that the problem lay within me. Never would I have to nerve to tell my father that I stopped liking his "famous macaroni surprise" when I was in kindergarten, or my mother that she didn't have to tell me I did great at a game when I knew I had always sucked at soccer. The flaws we hold. What to do with them? And what to do when they one day disappear?

The day that I met Claudia was the day I had just opened a fresh new diary. I still remember the exact way that the spine cracked open so that the pages kept flicking back in my face when I didn't hold them down, and the sparkly red cover with the three miniature hearts. It was a Tuesday afternoon. My mother had just scooped me up from piano lessons so I went to my room and began writing a new entry. I had only scribbled down the date when my mother reappeared in the doorway standing next to a woman I had never seen before. She was tall; about 6 foot, had a pale white complexion, and large protruding brown eyes.

"Ellen I'd like you to say hello to Claudia! She's going to be our new nanny." " She had said. "With the new job promotion things are going to get a little busier here honey, so Claudia will be giving us a hand around the house."
I distinctly remember trying to smile. It was forced and awkward. But fortunately for me, Claudia recognized this quite instantly and returned the same facial expression. I hated nothing more than fake people. Claudia nodded her head foreword in some sort of bow, turned around briskly and left the doorway. My mother looked puzzled in her direction.

"I hope you're not upset Elle, but Mom just really needs the extra help. And besides, Claudia can't speak a lot of English so she will be mainly just doing her job, getting it done and leaving again.

Does that sound okay?"

"Mom, it's fine." I replied bluntly. I didn't see Claudia anymore that day. I wrote a one-pager about the awkward, lanky woman who had stood in my doorway and greeted me like we were in Japan. It was simple, but satisfying.

My experiences with Claudia after that were nothing but strange. I'd wake up each morning to find she had become just another part of the weekly routine. I would sit at the table to find breakfast at 7:15, a packed lunch at 7:20 and a ride to school at 7:35. It seemed to be making my mother happier to have more time to do her own things. Claudia even brought me to Dad Days which were an entire half hour drive away. But what bothered me was the silence. Not once in an entire two weeks of being with her every day had she even as much as said hello. She just nodded. Always that same single nod.

But there was one thing I sure as hell loved about having the new nanny around- she always gave me great stories to write. The creepy middle-aged woman in my kitchen soon became the protagonist of the first good thing I had ever written. And I wrote it in that red sparkly diary. I began to make theories about where Claudia had come from. At first I had suspected she was an escaped refugee and ex-con from some foreign land across the world. Maybe she had stabbed a guy in Peru, drowned her own child, or walked shoe-less from Europe to escape an abusive husband. They all seemed like probable ways to make Claudia an exciting person. After all, the woman didn't speak. There had to be a reason why she didn't even as much as curse in her own native tongue while burning her hand on the kitchen stove. At the age of ten I had figured it all out. Claudia had some sort of tragic history and I just knew it! Did something so indefinably terrible happen to her that she had literally become mute?

Her usual time of departure was around 6 o'clock, which also happened to be the greatest hour of every single day. After 6 o'clock I never had a soccer practice, a piano lesson or an ice-cream date with Dad. It was my alone time. On the night that I finished off the final touches of the story about Claudia being a runaway circus freak, I crawled in bed, got tucked in by Mom and fell asleep. It was the first night I dreamt about Claudia.

I was facing the doorway as she entered. Her footsteps, like her, were so silent they near made her invisible to me. She walked across the room to the table where my diary lay; it was open to the page I had just finished, with a paperweight elephant propped on top. Although she was now behind me, I could still see everything that was happening, even with my eyes shut. With her hands outstretched over the book, she began to twist her fingers into curves as a strong white light came from the middle of her palm. I tried to roll over my body, sit up, stop her. But I was frozen into the position of sleep. My face still toward the doorway I had first seen her standing in. She then closed her hand into a fist, causing the paperweight elephant to shoot off the pages and the diary cover to shut.

I felt absolutely terrified inside. It seemed as though she had placed my body in some sort of trance where my mind was still capable of hearing and viewing everything that happened around me! I tried to press my lips apart. They were glued shut. My heart began beating faster and faster as Claudia walked to my bed and hovered above where I lay; paralyzed. She extended her hand over my face and did the same twisting motion with her fingers. It was the last thing I could remember.

The next morning I flew up straight in my bed. Looking over to where my diary had been the night before, I saw to my surprise that it was shut, with the sparkly cover now exposed. I went over and picked up the elephant from the floor and wrote a quick entry about the dream I had had the night before. I had never had a dream that felt so real, but it just couldn't have happened. After some pondering I went to greet Claudia good morning.

When I walked into the kitchen my mother did her usual extra-happy "Good morning Sweetheart!", and continued doing things about her way. Claudia was making grilled cheese sandwiches which I basically despised, but I grabbed a glass of OJ and sat at the table like a happy camper.

"Grilled cheese okay Elle?" Mom asked.

"It smells delightful!" My mother always liked using words like "delightful" to make herself sound grand. I opened my mouth to say "It's fine", but instead these words came out of my mouth that I had no control of! "I fucking HATE grilled cheese sandwiches!" I shouted. I cupped my hands over my mouth. So shocked at what had just happened I didn't even try to defend myself with an apology.

"Ellen!!" My mother hollered. "Where did you hear that horrid word? And how dare you be so rude to Claudia!"

"I... I... I don't know how I just said that." I mumbled.

"Get ready for school."

I looked at Claudia as she turned around from her place of cooking. She had a grin on her face from ear to ear, and the look sent a shiver down my spine. I had never cursed out loud before. A thought like that would always stay inside my head. I grabbed my things and caught the bus that morning.

Things only got weirder after that. Every day I would follow the weekly routine, come home and write a Claudia story, and later that night find myself dreaming the same repeated dream. She would walk into my room, place her glowing hand over my diary (wherever it happened to be), and then over me. At school I was finding it harder and harder to lie, especially about the simpler things. I was always well-known by teachers and family as "the polite girl". But now, I found I could not even lie about wanting to take the ice-cream order downstairs. I blurted out arrogant comments in class when Mrs.Slaney asked if everyone understood, I told my best friend that I hated when she wore her hair up cause it made her ears stick out, I even screamed at my piano teacher for commenting on my posture... again. It was hell.

After a week of my constant, uncontrollable bluntness, I decided that I should stop writing in the sparkly red diary. I figured I was making myself paranoid. After all, it was impossible that Claudia was even inside of my house at night, let alone her using some sort of superpower to read my diary. It had to be in my head just like the stories I was creating. So I chose to put the tales of Claudia to rest.

Unfortunately for me, although the stories had stopped the dreams continued. But they were quite different. Claudia would still walk silently into my room, but instead of her scanning my diary, she would sit on my chair and write in it. As she wrote she would speak in this language I had never heard of. Repeatedly she would say, "Xulr vit slaba yety" and close the diary. She then proceeded to stand over me and do her usual blessing, or whatever it was.

As weeks passed by, I began to have more and more difficulty with lying. Now, instead of not being able to lie about the small things, I couldn't lie at all! My mother had made me an appointment with a child psychologist, and cancelled the Dad Days. I kept overhearing her tell my grandmother she thought I was having "attachment problems". Things in my life were complicated sometimes with my parents being divorced, but I was over that long ago. She just couldn't understand. The teachers would continue to make concerned phone calls until I sorted this thing out! I couldn't control the bluntness. My mouth just said the words before I could stop them! But I knew better than to try and explain this to an adult.

What puzzled me the most was that even though Claudia had appeared to be writing in my diary each night, unlike before, there was no evidence of this. The pages were all blank. One morning, after having the dream again, I got up and immediately wrote down the phrase she spoke in the dream each night: "Xulr vit slaba yety". I practiced saying it for days with the intention of eventually speaking it to her and hopefully getting some sort of reaction. Dreams were, after all, only dreams. But one could never be sure. I had exhausted all other options and I was beginning to think that anything was possible. However, as crappy as it was to have everyone hate me for my honesty, I had gotten what I wanted. No longer was I in piano lessons or on a soccer team. Instead I took after school art!

One day my mother dropped me off at the house before going to pick up groceries. "Claudia should be home" She had said. And she most certainly was. With my mother absent for awhile, I recognized this as the perfect opportunity to be with Claudia alone, long enough to do what I had to do. I went straight to my bedroom, passing Claudia in the kitchen, and grabbed the diary from my shelf. Flicking to the blank page where I had written the phrase remembered so vividly from my dreams, I brought it to the kitchen. Smacking the open book down on the counter, I looked at Claudia and said, "Xulr vit slaba yety." What happened next was so unreal that I still, to this day twenty years later, cannot explain with perfect detail. Claudia smiled at me for a second and then took my two hands in hers. She then repeated the phrase I had said.

Frightened, my body froze. Not knowing what she would next say or do to me! But she just let go of my hands, took the journal and happily jumped her way to the kitchen table. I joined her. Looking back now, I have no idea why...

Claudia placed her right hand over the page where the words had been written just a few days before. And just like in my dream, she twisted her fingers above it and produced this bright white light. Suddenly, where the page had been blank, pictures began to appear. She then used her fingers to move the pages without touching them, exposing pages on top of pages of pictures. Drawn just as they had been in my dream. Each of them were of two creatures holding hands; one which was tall and the other short. The creatures were not people at all for they had distorted heads, with bulging foreheads. And scales... so many scales.

I looked at Claudia with petrified eyes as she again took my hands in hers.

"Se...See?" She said in English, with a smile on her face "Come-with-me-now."

I did not answer out of the fear of my own life, but it didn't make a difference. The next thing I knew Claudia reached her glowing hand foreword into my skull. There was a brief moment where the pain was so excruciating I prayed to God that I would die. I could feel her long, lanky fingers as they rooted inside of my skull. As she finally discovered the section of my brain she was looking for, my youthful bright blue eyes rolled to the back of my head and I collapsed to the floor. As a sharp sound shrilled through the air, Claudia remained standing. That same curious grin, was planted on her face.

My mother later came home to an empty kitchen. No Claudia. No me. No lies. I've tried so hard to continue my life as though my experiences with Claudia were part of a fictional story, made up by my child-self. Creating explanations for the impossible has never gotten me far, but at the age of 21 I still tell my story in the hopes that I will eventually meet someone as messed-up as myself. Insane enough to listen to the story of an alien babysitter. I don't expect you to believe me, or the stories I have recorded in that red, sparkly diary. But there is one thing that is for certain; I appreciate every white lie I am able to tell. After waking up at my father's house the following morning, with a frantic mother screaming at me to explain why I would ever run away from home, I had never felt more relieved to realize that I could tell her that Claudia wasn't there when she dropped me off that day. I said that I felt afraid to stay home alone, so the neighbor dropped me off on her way to the doctor. The look in my mother's face was memorable. There was relief.

I still see Claudia from time to time. She comes to me in my dreams at night, when I'm nestled in my bed sheets in a one-bedroom apartment, in a different town. She opens my door, creeps along the hardwood floors so silently, it's as if she can float. She stands over my bed as I open my eyes to her smiling face. She is holding a basket filled with god damn grilled cheese sandwiches. Freshly made, with a touch of love and slime.

# NOT YOUR ORDINARY
# LITTLE GREEN MEN
### By Kelli A. Wilkins

Sam walked into the kitchen and saw Margie spreading peanut butter on a cracker. He frowned. She had been acting strange ever since they moved into the house two weeks ago. "What are you doing?"

"Feeding the pixies. They're hungry."

He peeked out the kitchen window and looked around the back yard. "Is there a stray cat outside?"

Margie had the innate talent of attracting every stray critter in the neighborhood. Somehow, orphaned creatures always found her and knew that she'd adopt them. She was constantly feeding something that had wandered in off the street. That was how they'd gotten their latest cat, Muffin.

Sam let the curtain fall back into place and coughed as a cloud of dust went up his nose. "Wait a minute." He turned to her. "Did you say pixies?"

"Uh-huh." Margie nodded, her chestnut-colored hair bouncing on her shoulders.

"Okay... what is it, really?" he asked. "A mother cat and kittens?" Sometimes Margie kept the critters hidden away and gradually eased him into the idea of having a new pet. He glanced at the crackers and scowled. Cats didn't eat crackers.

Margie took the plate and headed down the narrow hallway that led to the main staircase.

"Hold it, hold it." He chased after her, tripping over unpacked boxes and buckets of cleaning supplies. "Is it a squirrel? A chipmunk?"

"No dear." She turned and batted her long lashes at him. "Pixies. I'll be back in a few minutes to help you in the dining room."

"Have you been in the wine?" he called out as she darted upstairs.

***

Sam sighed as he wandered into the spacious living room. The house was in shambles. Everywhere he looked, something needed to be cleaned, fixed, painted, or outright replaced.

What had he gotten himself into? Buying a fifteen-room Victorian monster at foreclosure had been a risky investment, but he couldn't pass it up. Margie had always had her heart set on running a quaint B&B in Maine. She grew up just outside of Lisbon Falls and she loved the countryside. After a little persuasion, Margie had convinced him to leave their hectic lives behind and open a B&B filled with antiques.

He'd never been able to resist Margie's charms. Besides, nobody in the local area wanted to buy the house. There were rumors going around town that it was haunted, and the old lady who had owned it was a kook.

Even after two weeks of constant work, he was still sorting through piles of junk. The old woman who had lived here might have been a little nutty, but she certainly had been a packrat.

He grabbed a handful of yellowed "Not of This World" newsletters and dumped them into a trash bag. Everywhere he looked, he found books and pulp magazines about UFOs, aliens, and mystical creatures.

"No wonder everyone thought the old lady was a wacko," he muttered. He glanced at the cover of a sci fi magazine. The poorly drawn illustration showed three little green men standing next to a rocket. He frowned. Maybe these magazines had given Margie the idea about the pixies, or maybe she'd been hearing the strange noises at night, too.

\*\*\*

"So what makes you think they're pixies and not gnomes?" Sam asked, as he applied a coat of walnut stain to the dining room floor. "Do we have any leprechauns running around? We really could use the luck."

"Don't make fun of them, Sam. They might be listening," Margie said, glancing around the empty dining room.

He paused with his paintbrush in mid-stroke. After ten years, he had learned to recognize the serious tone in Margie's voice. Whatever was going on, she was taking it seriously. "Have you been hearing strange sounds at night?"

He hated to admit it, but ever since they had moved in, he'd heard things. So far, he'd been able to dismiss the scrabbling sounds behind the walls and the shadowy movements he caught out of the corners of his eyes. After all, the house had stood empty for years. They probably had mice, squirrels, and miscellaneous other rodents running around.

Margie eyed him warily. "Noises? Like what?"

He continued staining the floor and tried to

sound casual. "Like something moving around. Maybe we have squirrels in the attic."

"Or pixies."

He rolled his eyes. "Oh, come on Margie. You've been reading too many of the old lady's sci fi magazines before you go to bed at night. There's no such thing as pixies. But supposing there were, where would they live?"

"In the dumbwaiter, so they can move around the house easier," she answered.

He crossed the room and raised the wooden door on the ancient dumbwaiter. "Hello! Pixies! Want some crackers?" he called out into the darkness.

Margie rushed to his side and tugged on his arm. "Don't tease them! You'll make them mad. They're shy and—"

"Booga, booga! Come out and play, pixies!" Sam looked up into the dumbwaiter shaft. "Ow! Damn!" He cursed as something splattered on his forehead. "What the—"

He wiped the sticky mass off his skin. Margie burst out laughing as he stared at the peanut butter-smeared cracker in his hand.

*\*\**

"I'm going to the store. Do you want anything?" Margie asked.

Sam yawned and nestled into the sofa cushions. "No. I'm fine right here." He was exhausted from working on the house all weekend. For some reason, Margie finished her work in a flash, while his projects were met with countless delays. If he were the paranoid sort, he'd swear that someone was playing tricks on him.

Yesterday he had left a paint scraper on the hall table and went into the kitchen for a glass of iced tea. When he returned, the scraper was gone. After wasting twenty minutes searching for it, he'd found it on top of the bookcase in the living room.

"Don't let Muffin upstairs, no matter how much she complains. She's been trying to get in the attic and—" Margie stopped. "You know."

"Do they have a room of their own?" he joked. Maybe Margie didn't want to admit that she was feeding chipmunks or other "cute" vermin that would have to be chased out of the house.

After the "cracker assault" on him yesterday, they had dropped the whole subject of pixies. He still wasn't sure how the cracker had fallen on his head, but part of him didn't want to know.

"Real funny," she said. "I'll be home in an

hour."

He closed his eyes and tuned out the television. He hadn't slept much last night. Something kept scurrying around in the walls, and once or twice he'd thought he heard odd whispers. Maybe the house was haunted. At least that was easier to believe than that it was infested with "wee folk."

A plaintive yowl interrupted his thoughts. Muffin was crying and clawing at the upstairs door. He tossed the remote control on the coffee table and rose from the couch. Muffin paced by the door, twitching her tail.

"You smell a mouse? Go on, bring it to Daddy." He opened the door and she raced up the stairs.

He returned to the living room and reached for the remote. The coffee table was bare.

"Now what the—" He scowled and looked under the table. Nothing. "Come on pixies, ghosts, whatever you are, that's not funny," he called out into the empty room. "Oh never mind!" He flopped on the couch and closed his eyes.

What seemed like seconds later, he was woken by a deep-throated snarl. He leapt off the couch and yelped in pain as he stepped on the remote control.

Muffin crept into the living room, growling.

She was carrying something in her mouth.

"Good girl! Let me see," he said.

Muffin released her struggling prey onto the carpet.

He leaned close and stifled a scream. Whatever Muffin had caught was no mouse or chipmunk. It was a–

"Honey, I'm home!"

He cringed as he heard the front door close. He glanced up just as Margie entered the room.

"I bought some… Oh my God!" She dropped the grocery bags and knelt in front of the small creature. She gently scooped it into her hands.

The five-inch tall being looked like a tiny person. Nearly translucent skin covered its thin arms and legs. It wore a white scrap of cloth that resembled a toga. The thing narrowed its huge amber eyes at him and blinked once.

Sam grabbed Muffin and stood up. "What is that *thing*? Is it okay?"

Margie nodded as the black-haired being started to move around. "Yes. He's just stunned." She looked up at him and frowned. "I told you about them, Sam. Why didn't you believe me?"

He stared at the creature in her hand and swallowed hard. "Trust me. From now on, I will."

***

Sam trailed behind Margie as he carried the huge box into the attic. "I'm sure they'll like it. It's better than a crate." He placed the box on the floor and slid it toward the attic crawlspace.

Ever since Muffin had caught the little "man" last week, he'd been trying to atone for not believing Margie. He had poured through the old books and science fiction magazines he'd found in the house. According to the literature the old lady had collected, pixies were supposed to be good to people who were kind to them. But if you got on their bad side…

He shuddered. What would these creatures be capable of if they were angered? They had dropped the cracker on his head as a playful warning. What could they do if they set their minds to causing real damage?

He didn't even want to think about that. There were stories in the old woman's pulp magazines about vengeful elves and sprites wreaking havoc on people who had done them wrong. And after seeing this little "creature" moving around, he didn't want to take any chances.

On Thursday, he and Margie had explored the attic and found a crawlspace half-hidden behind an old wardrobe. He had pulled away some of the plaster and uncovered their lair. They were living in two dirty crates and using scraps of old clothing as bedding.

"Sam, are you sure about this? They might not like it," Margie said.

"What's not to like?" He took the wooden Victorian-style dollhouse out of the box and eased it into the crawlspace. "No pixies of mine are going to live in poverty. Look, I bought some doll furniture and…"

He yelped and jumped back as one of the beings scurried out from behind a dusty tomato crate. Even though Margie insisted they were friendly, the sight of them still unnerved him. Whatever they were, they weren't natural.

Margie sighed. "Oh for heaven's sake, Sam! Let me, you'll scare them." She started to unpack the tiny pieces of furniture. "Why don't you see what's in that old trunk in the corner? There might be something we can use for them inside."

He opened the trunk and rooted around in the musty tablecloths and doilies. "Hey! I've got an idea! We can buy some doll clothes for them and—"

"And maybe a book at the pet shop called 'Pixies as Pets.'" Margie rolled her eyes. "They're not toys, Sam. All they want is to be left alone.

They were living here just fine on their own. They don't need us. We disturbed them."

"Well, I hope that once they're settled in we can…" His hand struck something hard at the bottom of the trunk and he pulled it out. "Look at this."

He opened the antique leather-bound book. "It looks like the old lady's diary. Leonelda Preston, 1919." He flipped through the yellowed pages. "Maybe the historical society would want it." He squinted at a page. The black ink was faded in spots, but he could still make out the words. "Hey, listen to this."

"'…strange orange lights in the night sky woke me late this evening. I heard an odd buzzing noise and went to the window. Something resembling a metal serving dish was half buried in the ground. It had sheared the top off the pink azalea.'"

He stopped reading.

"Go on," Margie whispered.

"'I crept outside and examined the peculiar object. To my horror, several tiny beings emerged from within. A fair-haired one carried another who appeared injured. They looked at me and scampered under the azalea. I thought I was dreaming or had gone mad. A lesser woman would have fainted from the sight. Certainly such things are not of this

Earth!'"

He arched an eyebrow and looked at Margie. "I told you we didn't have pixies." He chuckled and gestured toward the crawlspace. "We've got aliens."

# TELEPORTER
## *By Jennifer Caddell*

She didn't mean to fall in love. It was space camp after all. But there he was, sitting with the other space geniuses in physics, staring at her with so much intensity. Her heart stopped, her stomach twisted, her head swam in the depths of such passionate love. She couldn't ignore those feelings. She knew he was her soul mate; the only one she could possibly love. He held her hand on that very day, told her how much she affected him. They embraced and melted into each other's arms. She never wanted to let go.

Unfortunately the last day of camp arrived. His parents arrived first. They waited for him to say 'goodbye'.

"I don't want to lose you," Ryan clasped her hand and squeezed it. He wanted to kiss her, he wanted to wrap his arms around her small frame and feel her body against his. But his parents were watching, and he knew they wouldn't approve of such behavior. They were from the Kalonius Galaxy; 400 light-years from her home. He felt the evil weight of fate. They were too young to fly a spacecraft. Tears threatened their way into his eyes. He needed her. Needed her like he needed food and air.

Cassie wept when he released her hand. He whispered into her ear.

"I'll find a way. I promise." He kissed her ear and left.

They say that time heals all wounds, but this one could not heal. Cassie waited for weeks to hear any word from Ryan. She checked the mail, she checked her messages and she checked the hologram box. Nothing. Did he forget her?

But all was not lost. Another week passed when a message arrived in her hologram box. It was him! Cassie was thrilled when his face appeared within the box. He seemed distracted. He looked at her and gave a timid smile.

"Why haven't you written? Cassie asked

Ryan explained everything. He hadn't meant to take so long, but he was working on a way for them to be together. It would be dangerous, but it was the only hope they had. She stared at his image in wonder. What was he working on? What kind of miracle would bring them back into each other's arms?

"I can't say anything about it now. In fact, it's illegal." He looked around to see if anyone was close by. "Keep an eye out for me tomorrow, 3 am by your planet's time."

Cassie's heart pounded harder with anticipation.

"Where are we meeting?"

"Stand here."

"Here? Next to the hologram box?"

"Yes. I have to go now, someone is coming. I love you."

"I love you too." After his image faded, Cassie continued to stare at the box. What did he mean? How could he arrive here in person when he was hundreds of light years away? She refused to allow herself to hope. "I'll just wait and see what happens." She told herself.

*** 

Before going to bed the next evening, Cassie set her alarm to wake her up by 3am. However, she was too excited to sleep. She paced the floor in the dark, and tried to busy her mind on other things, but like a moth to a light, her thoughts flew back to him. What is he doing?  Was it illegal?  Did he steal a spacecraft?

Finally the time arrived.  Cassie was lying in her bed staring at the ceiling when the alarm beeped at her.  She quickly turned it off before it woke her parents and checked her reflection in the mirror. She wanted to be beautiful for him.  If he arrived.

The hologram box sat in a corner of the living room.  She walked over to the chair next to it and waited.

3:01. She checked the time every five seconds.

3:05. Where could he be?

Finally at 3:08 something caught her eye. She turned to stare at the hologram box.  It was glowing.  Little dots of light were spinning within the empty space.  She stared at it in wonder.  What was happening?  She had never seen anything like it before.  Her stomach twisted with nerves and excitement.  Was this him?  What was he doing?

A hand appeared from the center of the spinning lights.  It was his hand!

Cassie reached out and held his fingertips. She pulled at his hand revealing his arm, his elbow his shoulder, finally his head appeared out of the box.

"Keep pulling!"  He whispered.

Cassie grasped both his hands and pulled back. Eventually Ryan found himself lying on the floor in front of the hologram box. He made it! He stood up and surveyed himself.

"Yes! It worked!" He looked at Cassie. "I did it! I am here!"

Cassie gave him a huge hug. She buried her face into his soft shirt and breathed his scent into her lungs. He was really here. She could touch him, hear him, smell him. He was really here!

Ryan held Cassie for several minutes. They didn't say a word. They didn't need to say anything. Their hearts pounded a rhythm that stayed in sync during the entire embrace. They were meant for each other. Nothing would keep them apart. All of those days of utter anguish evaporated in this moment. His cheek against her head, hers against his chest, it was heaven.

"I missed you so much, my Cassie." Ryan finally broke the silence. "It was torture to be so far from you. Now we are only a few minutes away."

Cassie looked up at Ryan and smiled.

"I can't stay long. It is noon back at home and my parents will be looking for me soon. But I brought you something." He handed her a small device. It was a device with a single red button.

"This is for us to use. When you wish to be with me, point this remote at the box and click that red button. Leave the remote by the box. It needs to be here for when you come back. You'll see the universe spinning inside. Reach your hand through it, you will feel a tingling sensation and then you will feel the cool air in my room. I will pull you through the box."

"What is this?" Cassie turned the remote in her hand.

"A teleporter."

"What!" Cassie stared at Ryan in disbelief. "But teleporters aren't supposed to work! They are very dangerous!"

"I've been tweaking with this one and when I use it with the hologram box, it works perfectly. See?" He turned around in front of her. "I'm here aren't I?"

"That was very dangerous of you." Cassie smiled as she scolded him. Only Ryan would be smart enough to make his own teleporter. She embraced him again and sighed. She could never wish to be anywhere else.

"I have to go now. Let's do this again tomorrow. 2pm? It'll be 5am at my place."

Cassie thought. Her parents wouldn't be home until 5pm, so it would be a safe time to visit Ryan.

"Ok. I will see you then." They hugged again. Ryan bent down and touched his lips to hers.

Her mind went blank and her body ached for him even more.

"I love you." She whispered.

I love you too." He answered before plunging his head and arms into the hologram box. He eventually pulled the rest of his body through and disappeared into the spinning galaxy. Then the galaxy stopped spinning and the box was once again empty.

***

```
9am - Message from Ryan
Cassie, don't use the teleporter!
I'll explain later.
Love forever,
Ryan
```

Cassie paced the floor all morning. What happened? Why couldn't she go to see him? She felt terrible. She couldn't eat, her stomach was aching and turning every five minutes from her nerves.

2pm arrived and still no message from Ryan. Cassie felt exhausted waiting for a message from him. What was she supposed to do?

Meanwhile, Ryan had locked himself up in his room. His parents hadn't seen him all day. He told them that he felt ill and wanted to be left alone. Fortunately they were too busy to be suspicious and left for work. He looked at himself in the mirror.

"Oh God." He whispered as he stared at the hole where his ear used to be. How would he explain this to his parents? How would Cassie react? Would she no longer love him? He was afraid of her finding out. He should have known something like this would happen. Gifted scientists couldn't produce a teleporter that worked, why would he think his would be any different? He sat on his bed staring at his own hologram box. The box lit up.

"No! I told you not to come!" Ryan ran over and tried to push Cassie's hand back inside the box.

"Ryan! Help me!" Her distant voice echoed into his room. Ryan relented and pulled Cassie's hand to help her out of the box.

"What are you doing?" He shouted, "I told you not to come!"

"I was tired of waiting around, not knowing what was going on." Cassie said.

"The teleporter doesn't work. Look." He turned his head to show her the missing ear and prepared himself for her reaction.

"Oh Ryan! I am so sorry." Cassie tried to keep her composure. Would she return home with a missing ear too?

"I'll understand if you don't want to see me." Ryan turned back to look at her.

"I still love you, Ryan." Cassie hugged him to reassure him of her feelings. Ryan melted in her arms.

They spent that hour talking about their lives and hopes for a future together. Finally it was time for them to part once again. Before slipping back into the box, Cassie looked at Ryan. Fear reflected in her eyes. She wasn't sure if she would arrive home with anything missing, and she wasn't sure if this would be the last time they could be together. Ryan kissed her forehead.

"Send me a message as soon as you are home." He said.

"I love you." She replied and pulled herself through the spinning stars.

Ryan waited for some form of communication. What would happen to her?

Cassie arrived in her living room and pushed herself out of the box. She felt her head and was relieved that she had two ears even though one of them felt a bit odd. Then she felt the rest of her face. Two eyes, one nose, one mouth. All the parts seemed to be in place.

Cassie hurried over to her room to type a message to Ryan.

```
I'm back.  All body parts are
intact.  I miss you already.
Love endlessly,
Cassie
```

Ryan replied with relief.

***

Cassie's parents arrived that evening and while they were sitting to dinner, her mom noticed something was different about her daughter.

"Cassie?"

"Yes mom?"

"Where is your other earring?"

Cassie reached up to her ears and realized that one of her earrings was missing.

"Oh! I must have lost it when..." She stopped. She needed to think of a reason quickly. "… I was taking a shower."

"Hmm." Dad mumbled before taking another bite of dinner.

"You may want to check the tub for it before going to bed tonight sweetie." Mom was satisfied.

After dinner Cassie went into the bathroom and looked at her ear in the mirror. Not only was the earring missing, but there was no hole left either.

"Well, if the worst thing that happened is the need to pierce my ear again, then I can consider myself lucky." She grabbed a pin. Then she thought about Ryan and his missing ear. She felt bad that he didn't fare as well. She made a new hole, put on new earrings, and hurried out of the bathroom.

The next morning brought renewed desires to see each other again. Cassie checked for messages from Ryan. He said that his parents still haven't discovered his missing ear. He wanted to see her and was willing to sacrifice another body part to do so. Cassie warned him against it, but in the end, she wanted to see him just as much, and would have made the same sacrifice.

Ryan arrived that afternoon. Cassie surveyed him and noticed no other changes. They spent their time sitting on the couch together watching an action movie and kissing.

"This was definitely worth the danger." Ryan smiled down at Cassie. "I'd give my right arm to see you again!" He laughed, but Cassie couldn't. Her eyes expressed her concern for him. He held her again.

"We'll figure this thing out. Don't worry." Ryan disappeared through the box leaving Cassie behind to await his message.

```
Cassie,
I've arrived and believe it or
not, I have a new ear!  This one
has an earring though.  Very odd.
Love,
Ryan
```

Cassie sat, frozen to her seat. He had a new ear. A new ear with an earring! Her ear!! She wrote back.

```
Ryan,
That is my ear!  I think I have
your ear!  Sorry, but I pierced it
last night.

Love,
Cassie
```

Ryan didn't care. He was just happy that he had an ear back. He pulled the earring out of the ear and hoped his parents wouldn't notice the hole.

***

The next day brought another undying need to be together.  It was Cassie's turn to take the chance. When she arrived at Ryan's, she was perfectly fine but when she came home, her belly button was gone.  She wrote a message to Ryan and received his reply.

```
Cassie,
I think it would be best if we
visit twice each day.  That way,
we will only have swapped body
parts and hopefully our parents
won't notice.
Loving you,
Ryan
```

Cassie agreed so Ryan arrived, hugged his Cassie and left back to his house.  Cassie followed him home and came back with his belly button.  It was larger, and had a bit of t-shirt lint in it, but she didn't think her parents would notice.
Each new day brought them together.  After every visit, Cassie and Ryan would follow up with another trip through the teleporter, the trip that

swapped their missing parts. Cassie now had three of Ryan's fingers, five of his toes, and three teeth. So far all of these parts could be hidden from her parents.

"Do you think I will eventually turn into you?" She asked.

"I don't know." Ryan kissed her neck. "Maybe we will just keep swapping parts and end up with our own parts again." He didn't want to think about it. For now, he was happy to be with his one true love.

"Marry me." He whispered.

"What? Now?" Cassie pulled away from him. She wanted to look into his face, to see how sincere he was.

"Not now, but when we are adults." He kissed her nose.

"Yes, absolutely!"

It was Cassie's turn to go back home. She passed through the box and stood on the other side while waiting for Ryan to appear. When she pulled him out, he stood up to give her a hug before returning home. Ryan looked into her face and his heart sank.

"Cass. You are missing your nose!" Cassie reached up to feel her face. There was a hole where her nose should be. Her heart flew to her throat. Now there was no way to hide it from her parents.

She looked at Ryan. Her little, freckled nose was on his face.

"My parents will be home any minute." She said, "I need to go through and back in order to get your nose." Cassie dove into the box. Minutes later, she came back with Ryan's nose. It looked huge on her small face.

They stood there, staring at the other, trying to come up with a plan.

Suddenly, Cassie heard the front door open and the familiar jingle of keys.

"Hi sweetie! I'm home early, what would you like for...." Cassie's mom froze. There was a strange boy in her living room standing next to her daughter and neither one of them looked very happy.

Cassie turned away to hide her face. Ryan stood in front of her, guarding her from being seen.

"Hi Mrs. O'Pia." Ryan held out his hand.

"And you are?" Cassie's mom knew something was wrong, but she couldn't place it just yet.

"Ryan. Cass and I met while in space camp." He pulled his hand back. It was apparent Mrs. O'Pia wasn't going to shake it.

"Cassie, look at me." Her mom tried to look around Ryan. "NOW!"

Cassie jumped at her mother's command. She turned to look at her mom with tears in her eyes. This was it. The end of her life.

Cassie's mom screamed.

"What happened to your nose? What is going on here?" She grabbed at her daughter and pulled her closer.

Cassie and Ryan explained the whole thing: The teleporter, their love, their desire to get married. There was no reason to lie now. Not when the evidence was staring her mom in the face.

"Can she get her nose back?" Cassie's mom searched over her daughter. Her heart sank when she realized that little of her original daughter was left. Tears rolled down her face. "Oh Cassie, how could you do this? How could you destroy yourself like this?"

"I love him." Cassie started to cry.

"This is crazy." Mrs. O'Pia's face became stern. "Ryan, go home. I will see what Dr. Gram can do with you Cassie. But I think it is safe to say that the two of you are forbidden to EVER teleport again!"

Ryan tried to argue before Cassie's mom interrupted him.

"No! This is a nightmare! Go, now!" She yelled. Ryan looked at Cassie longingly before disappearing through the box.

***

```
Cassie
Our worst nightmare has come true.
I just overheard my parents
talking about destroying the
hologram.  They want to smash it
in front of me tomorrow morning.
I have an idea, but I am not sure
if it will work.  Can I come over
now?
Love, Ryan
```

Cassie's parents went to see Dr. Gram.  They didn't want her to be seen in public, so they brought a photo of her to the doctor's office.  She knew they wouldn't be back for another hour.

```
Ryan,
I only have an hour.  Hurry!
```

Ryan arrived and Cassie pulled him through the box.  He stood up and greeted Cassie with a shower of kisses.  Cassie pulled his body against her own and squeezed him. She didn't want to ever part from him again.

"This will be more dangerous than anything we've ever tried." Ryan held out his teleporter remote. Cassie's breath caught in her throat.

"Now you have no way of getting home!" Her stomach turned. There was no going back.

"Where is yours?" Cassie handed Ryan her remote. "We will take these with us together."

"Where?"

"There." Ryan nodded towards the hologram box. Cassie suddenly understood. He wanted them to go through the box together, without a destination point.

"What will happen to us?" She was almost too afraid to ask.

"I am not sure. If we take these with us, we have a chance of finding a destination, or.." His stomach turned.

"Or?" Cassie needed to hear the worst.

"We just float aimlessly forever." Ryan's hands grew cold and clammy with fear. "Shall we go?" Half of him wanted to leave, the other half was very afraid of what would happen.

Cassie heard the keys jingle in the front door. Her heart slammed against her chest. If her parents saw him, they would freak.

"Cassie?" Ryan whispered. His eyes were round with fear and desperation.

The front door opened. Cassie froze and stared at Ryan. It was now or never.

"Cassie! What is he doing here?" Cassie looked up in time to see her father reach for his stun ray.

"Let's go!" She and Ryan pushed through the box together. Before Cassie's parents could reach the hologram, they were gone.

Cassie's mother fell to the floor in tears. Where did her daughter go? What happened to her baby?

Cassie's father looked inside the hologram box. He furrowed his brows.

He reached into the box and pulled out two devices. Each one had a red button.

"What are these?"

# DANGER, MAYBE
### By Marian Powell

Danger. Maybe. Nothing immediate, just noise not normal for the mountainside. Sluggish with the overwhelming need to hibernate, she swung her heavy head from side to side, senses alert.

There, far away down the mountain, light glittered and flashed and she heard the strange, unnatural rumble of many shiny moving things. Not normal. Not normal equaled maybe danger. Glittering noisy things only occasionally moved along that strip of dark smooth rock that wound up the mountain. A shiny herd running up the mountain was not normal, was more like deer stampeded by the smell of a mountain lion. Very strange, and very strange, like not normal, equaled maybe danger.

Too far away to be a threat, her senses finally concluded. If not a danger then not of interest. She relaxed and her body, heavy with fat, demanded she stop moving and sleep.

Obeying her body, she turned and lumbered up the hill to the cave entrance. Here she paused, lifting her shaggy head to sniff the autumn air one last time, smelling and listening.

She heard and smelled a small party of humans on foot headed in her general direction, but that did not concern her much. As long as they stayed out of her cave, they could climb where they wished.

She could just barely squeeze her huge body into the cave entrance and down the narrow, twisting passageway to where it widened out to make a little room. Scraping the cave walls felt uncomfortable and so did having to go so deeply underground.

She had started a den under a rocky overhang but humans had come walking by, making noise. Even though they didn't notice her, she had felt she needed something more private and had selected this deep passage into the mountain. Here she had piled up a bed of bark and grass, leaves and moss. Not what she wanted but it would do for the winter.

Hardly had she settled her great bulk on the soft bed and closed her eyes when her ears and nose brought her reluctantly alert. Danger. She focused and realized humans were at the cave entrance, vocalizing loudly. Reluctant to heave her massive body up, she hesitated, sniffing. The smell of terror jolted her to her feet. Fear radiated down the passageway.

The humans had approached the cave in a panic. She had never before sensed this from people unless they were fleeing from her. These humans scrambling into her cave radiated terror. She had to learn what predator pursued them through the woods in case it followed them into her den.

She growled, a low, rumbling, warning sound as she squeezed her way forward into the uncomfortably narrow, winding passageway. A sudden silence ahead of her, then fear-laden exclamations. She lumbered forward, expecting the humans to run but when she emerged from the passage, they hovered near the entrance. Fear radiated towards her.

Gasps and shrieks when she appeared. The humans ran then, but not far. They paused halfway down the slope, all turning and pointing the same direction away from the cave, freezing like cornered rabbits.

Sniffing the air and listening, she couldn't detect any predator, yet the panic in the voices increased. She looked in the direction the frightened ones were pointing. Nothing. Her dim eyesight saw nothing until something streaked like distant lightning. Annoying. Not dangerous. She uttered a last warning growl at the humans, then turned, desperate to sleep.

The sky blazed up like a sun filling the world. She whimpered and tried to hurry to go deeper, away from the blinding light. Heat, intolerable heat followed. This was very strange. Dangerous. She scrambled forward until the twists and turns of the passage protected her. The strange wave of light and heat couldn't follow all the way to her den.

She started to settle down. Sound roared through the rocky walls, setting them trembling. She started up. This sound was louder and more penetrating than any she had ever experienced. The earth trembled as though a rock huge beyond imagining had slammed into it.

Nothing else happened until sometime after she almost relaxed into sleep. Her nose alerted her brain. Smoke. Smoke could mean danger. With extreme reluctance she rose and squeezed through the passage. Flame roared just beyond the cave entrance. She paused, ancient alarm burning through her blood. Heat blasted her, singeing her fur, while choking smoke filled her lungs. Whimpering, she backed hastily down the passage into her den. Wonderfully cold air soothed her as she turned around. A trickle of cold water on one wall eased the singed feeling.

She allowed herself the luxury of collapsing onto her bed of leaves and grass and bark. The ugly smoke still drifted in but no fire came with it. Fire grew outside. She was inside.

At last she could sink peacefully into hibernation, her system slowing and slowing, heart and breathing so sluggish that the fat stored in the cavern of her body would last her for months. Even the waste she slowly produced was recycled inside.

Her brain comprehended nothing of these facts. One small part of her brain stayed alert for danger but none came. Occasionally the cave floor trembled and she stirred but the tremors passed and she sank back into her all enveloping twilight place.

Finally an event happened that engaged some of her attention. Her body produced two cubs, one right after the other, so tiny in comparison to her that she needed to do nothing to birth them except be present, only half awake. Nonetheless, their tiny cries awakened her enough to tend them. She licked them all over, cleaning them, awakening and reassuring their little bodies that they were alive and that this was a good and safe world to be born into. She even turned on her side making it easier for them to suckle her life giving milk. She returned to sleep.

A little more of her brain stayed alert, aware of her babies' whimpers but only responding when necessary. The cubs grew larger day by day on the rich milk she produced out of her fat reserves. As they grew, her bulk began noticeably to shrink and her brain sent hazy images of an almost forgotten past.

Cubs. There had been cubs before these in some time past. She had no sense of how much time, only that somewhere there had been other sets of cubs, nursing and growing through the long, slow, dull winter while she slept.

Memories of aching hunger when the last of her fat had vanished and her body demanded she leave her den and feed. Feelings of overwhelming love and protectiveness, the need to stay with her cubs. Even stronger, the urgent need to leave them, to find food. She did not think those thoughts, only knew that she must leave, emerge into the bright spring sunlight and eat the tender new grass and leaves. Images filled her mind of a world of sunlight and new green growth.

She awoke, desperate now with the need to leave the den and find food.

Two large and playful cubs tumbled over her, delighted to have a fully aware mother. Growling at the bewildered cubs so they would stay, she lumbered quickly down the narrow passage, so thin now she could speed without brushing the walls.

Body memory of a painful blast of heat made her pause before the cave entrance, sniffing and listening. The air felt wonderfully cool with only traces of smoke. Carefully, she walked forward into gloomy darkness, looking for spilling sunlight and green growth.

No sunlight spilled down from the cloud infested sky. Old burn smells lingered, the wrong smell for spring. The world down the mountain showed only burnt out drab piles of ash and ruined trees. Desperate with hunger, she searched.

A little grass poked up here and there, struggling to grow in the dim light of a shrouded sun. She nibbled what she could and then she found a treasure trove of bones. The bones all turned out too burned to eat so she nosed about and then abandoned them. Finally, little scurrying beetles caught her attention. Desperately, she ate all she could. They and the scraggly grass provided an unsatisfactory meal but enough to let her return to her cubs.

Next morning, she hurried eagerly down the passage, desperate for food and light. Nothing had changed. The world still stood gray and gloomy and faintly smelling of old ashes. No sun. No fresh green smells. This world was wrong, did not fit the memory picture of life outside her cave. Therefore, the real world must be further down the mountainside. She must leave this area but that would take her too far from her babies.

Instinct rescued her, telling her to take the cubs with her, then wander far and not return to the den.

The cubs were delighted to follow her out into the unpleasant world. To them all was new and exciting, even chilly winds, piles of ash, burnt trees and old bones.

So she led them on a wandering downhill path, snatching a bite here and there of struggling grass, while expecting that a few more steps would bring her into sunlight spilling down on a world of lush grass and tender growth.

She wandered 'til the cubs began to tire and lag, too young for so long a trek. She flopped down on the ground to let them nurse, then, not smelling or hearing any predators, let them snuggle up against each other and sleep.

Sniffing the air brought the welcome scent of fresh water. A streamlet splashed down the mountain not far away. She drank deeply, discovered a number of tiny fish and beetles in and around the water. Having devoured all she could catch, she moved on for just ahead lay that strange flat black rock that wound down the mountain though it now had piles of ash and dust and here and there some of the metal things.

None of them moved.   Another piece of wrongness.  Then movement flickered across her sight and ears and her nose caught a multitude of scents.  Little scurrying creatures sheltered under the objects.  Memory pictures reminded her that when the objects were shiny and held people they also held food when they stopped.

The smell of rot reached her.  A whole system of life had grown up here over the winter. Food lived in the wreckage of the things that had been noisy and shiny, eating that which was rotting. It no longer mattered that she couldn't find the world of sunlight she expected.  Food and water existed here in this dark place.

She relaxed into contentment and called her cubs to wake up and join her.

# THE ROCKET SHIP
## *By Ian Lamberto*

I could hear him calling my name from upstairs.

"Johnny!" he shouted. "Johnny!"

I was in the living room, chasing cereal with my spoon while the T.V. blared. Beyond the window pane the blue sky beckoned, but until Mom got home from work, the park was out of bounds. My brother was still too young to be by himself, so from three to four in the afternoon, five days a week, the duty fell to me to watch him.

Sitting back, I turned up the volume.

"Johnny!" his voice cut through the scripted dialogue.

"What?" I finally responded.

"Come quick!"

"Why? What is it?"

"Come quick!" he repeated, his footsteps racing along the landing. "Hurry!"

Muting the T.V., I set the remote and my bowl on the table, and headed for the stairs.

"This better be good, Pete," I commented, loudly.

"It is! Hurry! You'll never guess what I made."

I stopped at the top step. "Another invention, huh?"

"Yeah, well, kinda," my brother answered from a room down the hall.

"Wonderful," I mumbled, recalling the last creation, the one that had started with matches, and ended with singeing both my eyebrows clean off. "Why don't you just tell me what it is?"

"You'll never believe me. You gotta see it."

My brother was wearing an old-fashioned pilot's helmet, with a scarf and goggles, and beside him was a large cardboard box. Stacked vertically, it rose halfway to the ceiling. Two oval windows had been drawn, one atop the other, and an opening had been cut, like a small door, into the base.

"All right," I said. "What's this then?"

His smile was beaming, and his hands were at his sides in a triumphant pose.

"This is my rocket ship."

"Rocket ship," I echoed, looking up at where the front cabin must be, fighting back a chuckle. "Right, right—"

"It took all week to build. But here it is, ready to launch."

"All week you say."

"Yup, and now we can explore the cosmos, and see new worlds, and meet new people, and learn all kinds of stuff."

No longer able to suppress the laughter, it burst from my throat.

"I'm serious," Pete yelled.

"Oh, I'm sure you are," I pretended to inspect the 'rocket ship.' "So, where are you going first?"

My brother paused, one eyebrow crooked.

"Come on," I said. "I'm curious, where?"

"Well since it's the trial run," he answered, slowly, then faster. "I think it would be best to keep it in orbit, you know, just in case."

"Makes sense, good idea."

His smile returned. "And so I've chartered a course for Winnipeg."

"Winnipeg? Why are you going to Winnipeg?"

He shrugged. "I like the name. And it's we."

"What?"

"It's we. Why are 'we' going? Not I, we."

"Okay, sure, Pete, um," I could feel the laugh once again rising. "When—when's lift-off?"

"A few minutes, just got to check the fuel intake," he tapped on a small square drawn on the side.

"Oh, and what kind of fuel does your rocket ship run on."

"Pure plutonium," he replied, matter-of-factly.

"Plutonium?"

"<u>Pure</u> plutonium."

"I see . . ."

"Yup, that was the trickiest part, getting enough, but we should be fine."

"Should be?" I crossed my arms in mock caution. "Are you sure?"

"No worries, Johnny. It's all set. So, what do you say?"

"Oh, I think I'll leave this flight to you, I've got some homework due tomorrow."

"We'll be back in time."

"Really, from Winnipeg," I snorted.

"Uh huh, plenty of time."

"Still, you should probably take this one alone. You could set a record for youngest pilot, right? And I wouldn't want to muddle that up for you."

"That's okay, I don't mind."

I walked to the doorway, waving with one hand, covering my snicker with the other. "No, no, you have fun. I'll catch the next lift-off. I promise."

"All right, then. Can you tell Mom where I went, I don't want her to worry."

"No problem. Oh, and send me a postcard won't you, from Winnipeg."

"You got it. See you later, Johnny."

"Good luck, Pete," and I left the room, shaking my head, rubbing a tear from my eye, as the laughter came through.

But, before I reached the stairs, a great noise filled the hallway. Like a car engine turning over, only ten times louder, it shook the walls and floor.

I covered my ears, running back to my brother's room, as a loud crash entered my bones.

"What is that?" I shouted, though the commotion had ceased. "What did you—?" I entered the doorway, my eyes widening to their breaking point. My brother was gone, his box was gone, and in their place was a dark, black, burn mark on the carpet, and above that was a circular gap of blue sky and splintered wood.

"No way . . . ," the words trailed out of my mouth, while I stared at a jet-stream steadily dissipating on the wind, only mildly aware of a door swinging open downstairs.

"Hello," my mom call. "Kids, I'm home, where are you?"

I knew I should be running to tell her what happened, to tell her to dial the police or the army, or whoever you dialed at a time like this, but all I could do was stand there and stare at the gaping hole in the ceiling, and wonder how far it was to Winnipeg.

# WE DON'T DO WINDSHIELDS
## *By Don Magin*

*COMMENTARY ON THE NEWS*
*FEBRUARY 13, 2031:*

Public reaction ran the gamut from "so-what" to plain old red-faced embarrassment to mad-as-hell anger. I guess I must fall somewhere between embarrassment and anger although I can't really see why we should be embarrassed, nor can I fully understand why we should be so angry. After all, what we were doing was good, but I guess nobody likes to be tricked into doing something, even if it turns out to be something good. Maybe that's what's embarrassing – that we were used (albeit for a worthwhile purpose), and somehow we should have known, or at least suspected.

I like to think of myself as a thorough news commentator, so I should present the facts I've dug out in my research before I comment on them.

Coincidentally, almost exactly 20 years ago the first advertisements appeared. Every possible form of commercial communication carried the ads, all over the world. The newspapers, the radio, the TV, the Internet, billboards, all carried the announcement:

> "NEW! 'SLIMR-U' The fast, easy, painless way to control your weight. So inexpensive that virtually everyone can look and feel their best – and their healthiest! No matter what or how much you eat! No exercise required! Available now by mail, and soon from selected outlets throughout the world."

That's it. That's the exact, complete wording of the first advertisement as I found it in the Jan. 17, 2011 issue of the Richmond, Virginia Times-News. Of course, it ran in virtually every other newspaper and magazine in the world on the same day. Radio and television carried the same words, along with the hoopla music and sound effects necessary to pull our consciousness to a level where we can separate the message from the news of the day, the top 40 songs, the soap operas and the idle chatter of announcers and DJ's. Banners with the same message popped up on the computer screens of anyone surfing the Internet, much to the amusement and annoyance of the surfers. Billboards suddenly blared the message to drivers along the highways and back roads in every country where billboards were still not banned. You couldn't miss it.

If it were some kind of ploy to heighten expectation that the ads said "now available by mail", yet no address was given, it worked. The ending human interest and information piece on almost all local and national news programs was on "SLIMR-U". Experts in the fields of nutrition, medicine, chemistry, biology, and numerous other health-related fields, repeated for millions of viewers that there can be no such thing as a "fast, easy painless" way to lose weight and maintain an ideal size "no matter what and how much you eat" with "no exercise". Calories consumed equals energy expended plus weight gain. Scientific, proven fact; that's that. Officials of the world's postal services publicly stated that selling any such device or diet plan through the mails would constitute mail fraud. The U.S. Food and Drug Administration, along with similar regulatory bodies throughout the world came down on the "SLIMR-U" as hard as might be expected, for nowhere in the world was any bureaucratic approval or license given to market such a thing. But the ads appeared again, a week later.

Soon after, the "SLIMR-U" devices began appearing. Some people had gotten them, told their friends, who got them, and on and on. Within two more weeks, testimonials began to appear in the newspapers, on radio and television, on the Internet, and even from street-corner soapboxes. "SLIMR-U" worked! How it worked, indeed <u>that</u> it worked was a mystery. Scientists from every recognized field (as well as from a couple of areas on the fringes of recognized science), were puzzled. No, not puzzled, but totally and absolutely stumped. "SLIMR-U" did work! But it couldn't. But it did. A disk, the approximate size of a quarter and weight of a dime, could trim people down to an ideal weight, and maintain that condition, regardless of how much or what the person ate, regardless of how much exercise or lack of exercise a person did.

And it seemed harmless enough. After all, a small disk that was placed on, not in, the body, on any patch of bare skin, outside or underneath clothing. Somehow, it stayed in place and could not be accidentally dislodged. Rain, snow, sunshine had no effect on it. It could be worn while swimming, showering, exercising (if you still happened to like that sort of activity), and just doing the ordinary things ordinary people do every ordinary day. It caused no allergic reaction – in fact you really never knew it was there. Except when you stepped on the scales. Yet it could be simply removed by the person wearing it, leaving no mark at all. What could be safer?

Medical science, even with its drastically stricter definition of safety could find no harmful effects. "SLIMR-U" did what it claimed, and no more. It even worked on animals. No more fat lazy pets. Dog or cat (or horse, or gerbil, or parakeet, or whatever) could be as sleek and trim as their owner. Not a bad investment for US$1.00. It was hard to believe then, back 20 years ago, and next to impossible to believe now, but the cost remained the same for twenty years – one dollar. Was it any wonder that virtually every adult person and domesticated animal wore a "SLIMR-U"? There was some early concern about its effect on children and normal necessary weight gain. Medical research on "SLIMR-U" of course did not stop just because it appeared safe and effective. It was soon discovered that the device did not prevent or hinder normal growth. Somehow, each "SLIMR-U" adjusted to the normal developmental metabolism of the wearer. Children who wore it still gained the proper amount of weight at the proper rate. Development from child through puberty to adolescence to adulthood was unaffected, except in a positive and healthy sense.

The physical sciences, too, took their best shots at "SLIMR-U". Logical reasoning was that before we could understand how it worked, we had to understand what it was. Chemists, physicists, biomedical engineers, and you-name-it scientists, were totally frustrated. Every technique of modern analysis in the book (and a few developed just for the purpose of examining "SLIMR-U") came up with the same results. The disk was a curiously ordered combination of elements, all of which were known to science. There was some aluminum, some tin, some magnesium, and minute amounts of lesser known elements, iridium, osmium, and samarium, to name a few. There were a few organo-metallic compounds bonded in some strange way, but their identity could not be determined. The consensus of opinion of world experts was that the "SLIMR-U" disk might be some sort of molecular electronic circuit. Instead of transistors, capacitors, and such, somehow proper manipulation at the atomic level of various elements could achieve what appeared to be a very efficient, low power electronic circuit. The organo-metallic compounds seem to be the link to the person's body systems through some sort of surface interaction at the skin. Beyond that, it could never be determined how the device worked, or even what it did to accomplish the weight loss and control.

This little device may have represented the proverbial kick-in-the-pants to technology to accomplish several major goals in solving world problems. Since people could now eat as much as they wanted and not become overweight, a major food source problem was accelerated. The perfecting of fish-farming techniques within 3 years after the introduction of "SLIMR-U" was the first major breakthrough. Kelp farming processing advancements followed that by a mere 6 months. Perhaps the greatest achievement came with the genetic manipulation of first rice, then other food plants, to enable them to grow in the nutrient-rich ocean bottoms, thereby effectively more than doubling the amount of "farmland" in the world. Technology quickly followed with sea-rice harvesters and other sea-farm equipment, as well as the development of communities of sea-farmhouses. These effectively eliminated the world hunger and living space problems, as many of the overcrowded and developing nations of the world leased huge numbers of these sea-farm communities. All of this was prompted by, and took place within 10 years of the introduction of "SLIMR-U".

Naturally, with such major problems as world hunger and overpopulation solved, and the mysteries of the oceans unveiled, technology turned its attention to the next great unknown, space. The lunar and Martian landing missions of the last decades of the twentieth century and into the new millennium paved the way for the joint effort of the United States, Russia, China and the European Space Federation to put the first permanent functioning space station in orbit midway between the earth and moon. This manned colony in near-space was of course where we were first contacted by (what translates to) the Space Alliance, which already counted 251 galactic life forms among its membership. We have no legitimate reason to be embarrassed though, because most if not all of the other members have existed for five to ten times as long as the human race.

One purpose of the Space Alliance is to share advances in technology. As fast as our space scientists and engineers can assimilate the knowledge, we are learning how to travel through space using the principles of matter-infrawave interconversion. I am no space scientist, but as explained to me, the speed of light is not an absolute limit to the velocity of a waveform, but merely a boundary condition, speeds beyond which are forbidden. As everyone who has taken elementary physics knows, "forbidden" does not mean "impossible". Earth "spacelists" (as these "space specialists" have been called) are just beginning to understand the principles founded on these "forbidden" laws of nature, and a very few of them have grasped the concepts thanks to the patient teaching of Space Alliance tutors. Travel through far distances in space is thus possible if the spaceship and its contents, including passengers, are transformed into infrawaves. The gravitational fields of planets, stars, asteroids and other celestial bodies can be used as effective "wave-guides", forming something analogous to the optical fibers or light-pipes through which light waves pass. However, as in the transmission of all waves, some energy is lost as the infrawaves pass on their journey. Although extremely efficient, even minute losses add up over hundreds of light years. Again, using the analogy of optical fibers, every so often, booster stations are necessary in order to preserve the information contained in the waves. Thus, engineering groups from the Space Alliance have had to scout possible new routes for their infrawave "roadways", finding appropriate locations for their booster stations.

Sometimes, it is necessary to prod a civilization toward a high enough level of technology to be useful to the Alliance. Earth is in a good spot. Just because Earth is where it is in the galaxy – an ideal spot for a booster station, somehow, humans were prompted to find solutions to world hunger and global living space. We humans have been accepted into undoubtedly the most elite alliance in the universe, and are being given the gift of long-range space travel. Talk about being in the right place at the right time!

What do we have to give in return? Only a little energy, to boost infrawave spaceships on their way. And not only don't we miss the energy, we gladly give it away, and have been doing so since early in 2011. Those little "SLIMR-U" disks are marvelous devices, but their prime purpose is not to control the weight gain or loss of the creatures wearing them. They do have unbelievably accurate control circuits that can monitor the body's energy needs, and permit the body to siphon off precisely the amount of energy it needs from its caloric input, but the real purpose of the disk is to capture the excess potential energy – that which usually winds up as fat – and convert it to infrawaves, which they broadcast to a point in space just past the moon. The small amount generated by each individual becomes rather significant when multiplied by the billions of people and animals on this planet of ours.

We are, and have been for the past 20 years, a booster station, an isolated filling station on a long barren road through the desert of space.

# THE HOUSE
# THAT DOOMSDAY BUILT
### *By Justin R Woolley*

I grew up here, in this stale world, this cold world without a sky. Concrete walls were my crib. Plastic floors were my playground.

I read a book once, before the books were locked away. It was about the world, the world outside. About plants taller than any man and animals that would run free in open spaces under the sky.

Imagine the sky. They say it is blue. How does anyone really know? No one here has seen it. Maybe it isn't even there. No. I must not think that, thoughts like these are forbidden. Sometimes though I cannot help but wonder maybe this compound is the entire world. I hope that is not so, it would seem a cruel joke top long to see a sky that does not exist.

There has been talk for years now, as long as I can remember, that we would be the first, the first to see the sky. The council says the doors will open when the world is ready for us to return, when it is safe. Safe from what? I would ask as a child. Safe from what? A question that I still ask now.

The council say that the reason we cannot leave this place is our fault, people I mean. People ruined the world. It doesn't seem fair to me, none of us were even born but we suffer this sky-less fate all the same. No one really knows exactly what happened but there are stories. There was a war. It began with war and it ended with winter, endless winter. The oracle would know the truth, if only we were free to ask.

I'm going to see the oracle now. The oracle is everything to us, knowledge and protection. She exists that we might live. She even turns on the daylight. I hope she will impart great wisdom to me. Today is my twenty-first birthday. I am coming of age and like all those before me I will see the oracle this day.

The guardian priests of the oracle, dressed in their white robes, hurry me into a small red chamber. As the door shuts behind me I stand still, as I was told. After the curtain of white steam disappears the door before me opens and I am nudged forward. I step into a room so white that I do not know where the walls end and the ceiling begins. Perhaps this is what the sky is like.

The guardians of the oracle tell me where to stand; they tell me what to say and what I am forbidden to say. I must not offend the oracle. The guardians of the oracle turn to me, "You will stand within the circle and have your time with the oracle. The time is yours and yours alone." The guardians retreat back through the door and it closes and I am alone, in white.

I must stand within the circle so that she can see me. I walk forward until I find it on the floor, it glows a dull green and it says 'interface'. I do not know what this means but I do as I am told and I stand within the circle.

"Interface loading" says an angelic voice from on high. They must be calling to her, calling the oracle out from her slumber. I suddenly feel guilty. I do not wish to wake the oracle if it would displease her, she turns on the daytime. I would not like there to be no daytime.

The room vibrates ever so slightly as before me a great clear arc descends from somewhere above, a strange altar rising from the ground before it.

"Sentient A.I. initiated, stand by."

More words I do not understand but as it says I stand. I stand in the green circle.

Suddenly she appears before me like a ghost. She is beautiful. Her slender eyes stare blankly into mine; she is smiling. I am frozen before the great oracle as she does nothing but stare at me. I am frightened as I stand before Her. She speaks.

"Good afternoon, stand by for retinal scan."

The oracle covers my face in her light, I do not move.

"No user record found in database, do you wish to create a profile?"

"Yes," I say, though I do not understand the question.

"Stand by."

"I am standing," I say, in case she cannot see me.

"Please state your name."

"My name is Emil Ricard son of Gareth Ricard."

"Good afternoon Emil Ricard son of Gareth Ricard your profile has been loaded with default administrator settings."

I stand still, the oracle is addressing me. We both stand and stare at each other for some time before I realize she wants me to speak. I'm not sure how much time I have or what I should ask.

"Is the sky blue?"

The oracle stares at me. I instantly know I have done wrong. I have disobeyed the guardians and spoken to the oracle about the world outside.

"Query: keywords, sky and blue. Basic explanation: The sky is a colloquial term for the appearance of the atmosphere. The atmosphere is the mixture of gas molecule surrounding the earth. It is primarily composed of the gaseous forms of nitrogen, 78% and oxygen, 21%. When light travelling through the atmosphere strikes gas molecules the process of Rayleigh scattering takes place. Primarily the shorter wavelength light is absorbed by the atmospheric molecules and radiated as frequencies seen as blue in the visual spectrum."

The door to the white room begins to open. The guardians are coming in.

"Emil Ricard, you have spoken to the oracle of forbidden topics you shall accompany us to the council." The guardian says as he waits for the second door to open.

"You said this way my time alone," I say to the guardian and to the oracle, "Please, let me learn, we need to know of the world."

"You will come with me," says the guardian as the door begins to open.

"No," I shout, "Oracle please close the door."

"Administrator privileges accepted clean room door locking."

The door slams shut on the guardian, I hear him banging but I turn back to the oracle. She must want me to learn.

"Please," I say. "When will we see the sky?"

"The sky is not visible from within the compound."

I turn and look back at the door, the dull thudding continues and I can hear muffled voices.

"Open the door Emil,"

"Oracle, I want to go outside."

"External sensors are malfunctioning; current radiation level is unable to be determined. Calculations based on radiological dissipation trend data indicate a 98% probability that radiation levels will be within safety margins. A manual external reading is recommended." The oracle says, I am growing frustrated, I do not understand what she is saying, only that I think she wants me to go outside.

"I will go outside Oracle."

"Stand by. Begin external excursion protocol. Ensure CBRN suits are sealed correctly before entering airlock. "

A red light begins to flash as a door behind me opens in the white. I go through, ignoring the banging of the guardians. Before me is a room I have never seen, I thought I had been everywhere in my world. It is a small silver room. I am trapped inside as the door closes behind me. Suddenly I feel as if I am moving. The small room I am in slides upwards. I must be going to the sky.

When the room stops and the doors open I step out, through the same doors but into a different place, a long corridor.

My footsteps echo as I walk, I don't think anyone has been here for a very long time. At the end of the corridor is a sign, 'airlock', a word I recognize. The Oracle had said to go through the airlock. But how can one lock the air?

I press the button beside the door and I step inside. The door shuts with a heavy thud followed by a sharp click.

"Ensure CBRN suits are sealed and oxygen supply is contained and uncompromised," says the heavenly voice of the oracle, "confirm when ready to continue."

"I am ready oracle," I tell her, "I am ready to go into the world outside."

"Prepare for external excursion."

There is a great hiss and my ears hurt. I collapse to my knees, grabbing at the sides of my head. I try to cry out but I find that I have no breath. I land on my side, gasping, but the air does not come. I am sorry oracle. I am sorry for whatever I have done that you feel I must be punished.

"I am sorry," I try to say but I don't think she can hear me and as I close my eyes for what must be the last time I feel a great rush of air across my face. I inhale deeply, my lungs burn. It is then I realize that the oracle tests me. She must be convinced that I am pure of heart, that I am truly the one to lead us outside.

The door before me opens. In front of me are steps, ancient steps cut from the very rock of the earth as the tunnel stretches upwards. As I climb the steps I see a door. An old wooden door surrounded by the brightest light. I try the handle but the door does not move, stuck with the years. I step back and kick the door with all my might until it crashes open.

The light is so bright that it blinds me, my eyes squint involuntarily. Through the haze of the water in my eyes I slowly start to see. I slowly start to see the real world. I look upward and I see the sky and it is blue.

# JOURNEY TO THE SURFACE
### *By Dixie Sorensen*

"If you look above you, you'll notice our domed sky which…"

"Sky? You can't see the sky from here," a young woman in her mid twenties interrupted. She had short brown hair and was clasping hands with her tall, dark-haired husband.

"Not the same kind of sky you are used to. I believe on land you would call it a ceiling, but here in the Trench, we call it our sky."

"But it can't possibly be made of air and atmosphere and everything else," the woman continued.

Commander Kim Johnson sighed. "Who gave you your initial briefing on land?" she asked, already knowing the answer.

The woman looked at her husband. "Zatos," he answered. "Brandon Zatos."

Kim frowned. Brandon was the type of recruiter who did it for the money, not because he believed it would save the world someday. "As I was saying, the sky, or ceiling, protects us from the tremendous amounts of pressure that would normally not allow life to exist this deep in the ocean. The light we have during the day is created there, and turned off for the night. The ceiling is full of filters and fans that control the purity and temperature of the water inside our city. It also regulates the amount of oxygen, and is basically the only reason we can sustain life here."

"How does it work, exactly," the man asked.

"We have a teams of experts who are constantly monitoring everything that goes on, and they would be the ones to ask for details."

"Don't you know?"

"Of course I do," Commander Johnson said briskly. "It is just too complicated to spend time discussing it now. I'm supposed to be giving you a tour."

"We really are in the Mariana Trench," the husband said skeptically. "As in the deepest part of the world."

"The very place," Kim answered. She pushed herself off the ground with her bare feet and floated in the water above her. "If you'll follow me, we'll continue your tour," she called.

The couple hesitated, not used to swimming everywhere they went.

"Swimming is much faster than walking," Kim assured them as they cautiously followed.

She led them to what appeared to be a residential street, although none of the houses rested on the ground. They floated at different levels, some close to the ocean floor, others near the sky.

She smiled as the couple's jaws dropped. Kim's favorite part of giving tours was seeing people's reactions to the floating houses.

"We adjust them with weights," she explained in her best commander's voice. "The elderly usually prefer to have their houses close to the ground, but the young and adventurous enjoy the lofty view."

The woman glanced at a house high above the ground and then at her husband. She lovingly leaned her head on his shoulder and winced. Her hand went to her neck where stitches formed a small ring.

"The gills take a while getting used to," Kim told her. "But soon you'll never understand how you survived without them."

"It's just so strange," the woman admitted. "I still don't understand how this is possible, the gills or the voice thing."

Her husband nodded. "I can't believe I'm speaking underwater."

Kim nodded and adopted her commander posture as she spoke. "The wire connects your larynx to your ear and can send and receive what I believe you call radio waves on land."

"Amazing," the woman breathed.

"I only know the basics," Kim admitted. "But when I take you back to the hospital at the end of our tour, you can ask Dr. Hansen while he checks your gills."

"Checks our gills?"

"To make sure transplant was successful. You'd die if they stopped working, so the doctor prefers to double check and triple check his work. He's been here long enough to know…"

"Commander Johnson," a loud voice called.

Kim twirled in the water to see a man in the same gray uniform that she wore swimming toward her. He had a small insignia on his chest that denoted his rank as a lieutenant.

"Commander, the General sent me to find you. He wants you to meet him in his office in ten minutes."

"Lieutenant, I'm currently giving our newest residents a tour of our city."

"The General sent me to take your place."

"Be sure to show them main street and the museum," Kim told him sharply. "And Dr. Hansen expects them back at the hospital promptly at five."

The lieutenant saluted as Kim propelled herself forward.

She reached the gray door that led to the General's office a few minutes later. Where the doorknob should have been, a small computer screen was sitting idly. "Commander Kimberly Johnson," she said in a loud, clear voice, placing her right palm on the computer screen.

The door swung open before her.

"Ah, Johnson," the General said distractedly when she walked in. He pointed to a chair across from his desk.

The room was small, but compact. The walls were the same gray as Kim's uniform, and various computer screens were displayed. A large oval desk sat in the center of the room. Kim took her seat.

She smoothed her long auburn hair against her skull, and watched the aging man, the founder of their city beneath the sea. His dark brown eyes were tired and his face was lined with wrinkles. Kim waited patiently, filled with respect for the General.

"Thank you for coming," the General said, sitting down in his chair.

"I wasn't expecting you to call me, sir," Kim told him. "I was giving the new couple a tour."

The General nodded distractedly.

"When will the next vessel arrive?" Kim asked when the General said nothing.

"That's why I've called you here," the General said, gazing up to meet her eyes. Kim could see the great burden he carried reflected in them. "We should have had two vessels since the one with your couple on it, and one more today. All three have failed to arrive."

Kim was immediately alert. "Are you planning to send a search party?" She had participated in two search parties while she had still been a lieutenant, and she wasn't eager to attempt another. Special suits had been designed to allow swimmers to leave the safety of the sky, but the pressure of the water was still almost too much for a human to bear.

The General shook his head. "That isn't my only problem," he said.

Concern shadowed Kim's face as she watched her commander. He seemed visibly weighed down by the news he was about to tell her. "I haven't been able to contact anyone on land for three weeks now. I thought at first that it might be our end of the connection, but I've tried the emergency wire line and sent a team of divers almost to the surface. They returned today with reports that all is in excellent condition."

"What do you think happened, sir?"

"Something is wrong on land."

Kim waited, wondering what that would mean for her.

"I'm sending a team to the surface, and I would like you to lead it."

Kim's eyes widened as she tried, but failed, to speak.

"I know you're only twenty-five, but you're one of my best officers, and I know you're up to the challenge," the General continued. "I've put together a team for you. Professor Levi Milborn, one of our best scientists, will be your consultant. I've also arranged for Captain Allen to control the surface vessel that will take you to land, along with Charlie Benson, a recent settler who is still familiar with life on land, and Ned Olsen, a government representative to handle the transactions with the land government."

"General," Kim sputtered, finding her voice. "I've never been to the surface before. I was born here, remember."

"I know, Commander. You were our first birth beneath the sea, one of our most successful experiments."

Kim was used to being referred to as an experiment. Her parents had been two of the first pioneers to journey to the Mariana Trench with the General. They had been allowed to be the first couple to attempt to start a family. Kim's successful birth had opened the door to many new colonizers.

"I'm not sure I should be the one to lead this expedition," Kim insisted. "Wouldn't one of the commanders who came from land be better?"

"Johnson, I need you to be a test for a new experiment once again. It is important to know if someone born here and accustomed to our lifestyle can survive there."

Kim's mouth tightened.

"Dr. Hansen assures me that your gills have not damaged your respiratory system, and that natural instincts ought to force it into action when you break the surface."

"And if I can't breathe?"

"Jump back into the water until the rest of the crew has completed the mission."

"Yes, sir," Kim frowned.

"Commander, I don't know what to tell you to expect. Life on land has worsened in the last decade. Most people here don't know it, but the atmosphere is almost completely burned away over Asia, Europe and Africa. South America has become so hot that it is impossible to live there. North America is the only land left that is able to sustain life, and the east coast is quickly becoming too dangerous. I'm sure you've noticed the increased numbers of immigrants in the last six months. The President of the United States, who is governing the entire land population now, has been communicating with me almost daily for a year. The world is ending, Commander, and life in the Trench is the only place that human beings are going to be able to survive. Communication with land is the only way we're going to be able to transport the people safely here before the world ends completely."

"General, what if the world has already ended?" Kim asked, hints of horror and awe in her voice.

"What if, indeed," the General muttered. "What if we are the only people left on Earth, Johnson?"

"I'll find out, sir," Kim assured him.

"I'm trusting you to do just that," the General said, standing up.

Kim snapped to attention, saluting.

"Your vessel leaves tomorrow morning from the launch pad in the sky. Six o'clock sharp. And Johnson, good luck."

***

"Surface in two minutes," Captain Allen, the commander of the surface vessel, called loudly.

Kim stepped to his side, glancing out of the small window. The water was clean and blue, and more transparent than any water she had ever seen outside of the city.

Charlie Benson, who had only been in the Trench for a few weeks, stood next to her, looking longingly at the clear water above him. "Nothing like breathing air, Commander," he sighed.

Kim was ready to try anything if it meant escaping the confines of the vessel that had been her home for the last sixteen hours. It was full of water, and designed like a submarine with extra thick walls to withstand the pressure of the deep. It had two floors, the top for the passengers, and the bottom for the controls. It was small and cramped, especially with five passengers.

They sped higher and higher until the water ended suddenly and they bobbed to the surface. The Captain pulled a few levers and disengaged the motor. Flotation devices sprang from the sides of the vessel, preventing it from sinking back into the ocean.

"Open the hatch," Captain Allen called from bellow.

Ned Olsen, assistant to the President of the Trench, climbed the ladder in the center of the vessel and pushed the hatch slowly open. "To the top," he said with a smile. Ned had only lived in the Trench for three years, and he was eager to see land again.

Professor Milborn, a small, frail looking man stood next to Kim and nodded at her. "Up to the surface and take your first breath, Commander."

Kim nodded, feeling butterflies in her stomach. She took one last gulp of water and propelled herself to the top of the vessel. She pulled herself up onto the edge of the hatch. Her gills immediately gulped for water, but there wasn't any. She clutched her chest as her lungs began to burn. She opened her mouth, unsure how to breathe something that wasn't liquid as her face slowly began turning purple.

"Breathe, Commander," Charlie shouted, slapping her back hard.

Kim's lungs were burning as she tried to gulp the air.

"Use your nose," Charlie urged, looking worried.

Kim closed her mouth as her head began to spin.

Charlie shook her shoulders. "Breathe," he commanded again.

Kim started to feel dizzy as she inhaled sharply. The relief to her lungs was immediate. Her head began to clear as she breathed again. Then the coughing began. Water spewed from her mouth, and her lungs started to burn again.

"Your lungs won't work on land if they're full of water," Professor Milborn explained coughing up the occasional mouthful of water next to her.

Kim cracked her eyes open a little bit, and quickly shut them again, still breathing hard.

"I'm blind," she muttered. "My eyes don't work on land."

"You don't have to wear your contacts on land," the professor explained. "Air doesn't hurt your eyes like water does."

Kim reached up to her eyes, feeling the clear contacts that she had worn since the day she was born. They were a part of her.

"I can't, Professor. I think mine are permanent now."

"They aren't," he assured her. "Take them out."

Kim reached up cautiously and removed one contact. She cracked her eye open, and blinked furiously. "This feels so strange," she mumbled, removing the other contact.

She opened both her eyes, and gasped. She could see. The light was brighter than anything she'd ever experienced before, but the view of the vast ocean kept her eyes from closing for long.

"It's different to see the water from above it rather than among it," Captain Allen remarked, climbing the ladder to join them.

Kim waved her hand through the air. "It's so light," she wondered. "It's like there isn't even anything there. I'll bet it's easier to move through the air than through the water."

Charlie laughed. "It's just air, Commander. Nothing special."

"It is if you've never seen it before," Kim disagreed.

"I think the General will be happy to know that you can breathe, Commander Johnson," Ned smiled.

"This water is too warm," the Professor muttered, running his hands through the ocean. "We need to get to the land," he said, looking at Captain Allen.

"We're in the middle of the Pacific Ocean right now, and we need to go north east to reach the coast of California. We should be there in about three hours."

He started the engine of the vessel again and pulled a few more levers. Propellers appeared on the side of the vessel, thrusting it forward quickly. The passengers descended back into the hold, standing in water chest deep and exploring the new feeling of breathing air.

***

"Land approaching," Captain Allen called.

The four passengers climbed out the hatch again, peering toward the approaching horizon where the land was slowly taking shape.

"Commander, you'll want these," the professor said, handing Kim a pair of soggy tennis shoes.

Kim looked at them curiously. "Shoes? I've never worn shoes before in my life."

"You'll want to now," Charlie assured her. "You can't walk on land without them."

Kim slid them on her feet, hating the feeling of confined toes. "Professor, am I feeling the sun?" she asked, running her hands over her bare arms.

The Professor nodded. "It shouldn't be this warm," he said again. "It's all wrong. It's going to burn our skin."

Kim looked at him with wide eyes. "It can't. Humans have survived here for years."

"Look at the sky," Professor Milborn ordered.

Kim glanced up above her. "I thought it was supposed to be blue," she remarked, glancing at the red blanket above her that was so different from her own man-made sky.

"It was, once."

"It wasn't this red last time I was here," Charlie announced. "It just had a pink tint."

"The atmosphere is almost gone," the Professor announced. "We have to hurry, or the world will end before we're ready."

Kim's question to the General rang in her mind. "Professor, what if it already has?"

"Then we have a large responsibility placed on our shoulders, Commander. We will be the only people left to keep the human race alive."

Kim shuddered. "How long until we reach the shore, Captain?"

"Four minutes," Captain Allen called from below.

The four passengers watched the land approaching as the sun quickly dried their wet clothing. "It looks so desolate," Charlie remarked, seeing the dull buildings that rose into the air.

"We should be docking right in the San Francisco Bay," Captain Allen called, looking at his computer screen. "Right...now."

They felt the bottom of the vessel drag in the sandy bottom below, and the Captain cut the engine again. The passengers descended to the control floor as the side door swung open, draining the last of the water from the vessel. Cautiously, they stepped onto the land.

"It's so solid," Kim remarked, surprised that the sand didn't flow away from her feet.

Charlie laughed. "Sand is the least solid ground we walk on here. Wait until I show you pavement and sidewalks.

"Look," the Professor said, his voice serious. The great city of San Francisco loomed before them, but it appeared empty.

Kim wanted to get a closer look, and tried to push herself off the ground and into the air. She fell flat on her face.

Charlie and Ned laughed out loud, and the Professor and Captain both had trouble hiding their smiles. "Walking is the only way to travel here unless you have a car," Charlie laughed. "No floating."

Kim's face was red as she pulled herself back to her feet. She began walking stiffly forward. Used to the restraints of walking through water, she was surprised at how easily her body moved through the air.

"It's too quiet," the Professor remarked. "Where is the noise of traffic and people?"

The ground changed as they reached the end of the beach and began walking down the pavement. Kim glanced around at the vacant houses that were all resting snuggly on the ground.

"I could never live here," Kim said. "The houses are so close together."

Charlie laughed again.

"Professor, look over there," Ned pointed.

An automobile was parked next to the curb with something black and charred in the driver's seat.

The Professor held up a hand as he stepped forward to peer inside the window.

"Human," he announced. "Completely burned."

Kim averted her eyes. Fire and burning were things she had only read about, and she had no desire to understand them any better than she already did.

"What do we do?" Charlie asked with worry.

"Split up," Kim ordered. "Search for survivors. Meet back here in two hours."

The Professor glanced at the sky with a worried expression, but said nothing.

Kim traveled north, combing through side streets and calling out into the buildings. Except for the echo her voice created, everything was eerily silent. She passed several blackened corpses, but she carefully avoided looking too hard at them.

She noticed the wonders of land life, itching to try to run an automobile or to explore a sky scraper. She wanted to understand the concrete beneath her feet and the sun beating down mercilessly on her skin, but the emptiness was too eerie to allow her to stop for long.

She flinched when she heard footsteps on her way back to the beach, but it was only Captain Allen. "Anything?" she asked as he neared her.

The Captain shook his head. "No life."

Kim nodded. "Same here."

"Commander, look at your skin," Captain Allen said, frowning at her. Kim glanced down at her arms, which were a vivid red. She put her finger tips on her forearm and nearly screamed. Her arm was hot and burned when her fingers touched it.

"What's happening?" she asked, noticing that the Captain's skin was also bright red.

"We're burning," he said, glancing at the sun, which glowed red. "Back to the vessel."

Kim ran, her tennis shoes squeezing her toes worse than before. Charlie was already waiting at the beach when she arrived, but the Professor and Ned were still missing.

"To the water," the Captain shouted, running towards the ocean.

The three barreled into the vessel, closing the hatch above them, sealing off the merciless sun.

"Which way did the Professor go?" Kim asked, seeing Ned running down a side street towards the beach.

Charlie pointed east, and Kim dashed back out of the vessel, feeling the heat of the sun immediately begin to attack her again.

"Commander Johnson," Captain Allen called. "Come back here. It will burn you!"

Kim ignored him, running east. Her chest heaved as she dashed around buildings. "Professor," she shouted loudly.

She heard a noise down an alleyway and sped forward. She turned down the street and saw the professor leaning against a building.

"Professor," she called, but he didn't turn.

She dashed to his side, breathing heavily.

The Professor's frail skin was blood-red and beginning to crack.

"Professor, you can't stay here. We're all burning."

He didn't respond. Kim gritted her teeth and threw the Professor over her shoulder. She tried running again, but could only manage a brisk jog with the Professor weighing her down.

Her face burned as she felt the sun trying to stop her from reaching the vessel.

The beach came into view, but her breathing forced her to slow her pace. The Professor stirred on her shoulder.

"Captain," she shouted as loud as she could. "I've got him."

She tried jogging again as the rows of buildings began to end.

The Captain and Charlie dashed out of the vessel towards them. Kim pushed herself harder as she reached the sand. Charlie took the Professor from her, and they all dashed for the vessel.

Ned swung the door open as they reached it. Together, they lifted the Professor to the upper level.

"Captain, get us underwater," Kim ordered like the commander she was.

Captain Allen descended to the controls, and the engine started. The vessel jolted as it tore away from the sandy beach and was propelled across the surface of the ocean.

"Under," Kim shouted impatiently.

"We can't go under until we're in deeper water," the Captain shouted back.

Kim glanced with worry at the Professor. His breathing was shallow, and his eyes were still closed. "What can we do for him?" she asked, unfamiliar with burns and the sun.

Charlie shrugged when her eyes fell on him. "We used to get sunburns, but nothing like this. I don't know what to do."

The vessel jolted again as the flotation devices were retracted and it started to sink into the water. The bottom level began to fill with water. "Pray that our gills still work," Kim muttered, as she felt the Professor's forehead.

Soon, the water started to rise to the upper floor and wash over the Professor's torso, leaving only his head free.

"Come on, Professor," Kim whispered, holding his head.

The Professor took one shuttering breath, and then stopped breathing. His head went limp.

"NO!" Kim shouted, shoving his head bellow the water and pushing water into his gills. "Breathe, Professor," she shouted while Ned and Charlie looked beyond her shoulder. She moved the Professor back and forth in the rising water, ignoring the searing pain that was rippling through her skin at every movement. "Water is going in his gills. He should be breathing!"

The water had risen to her chest. "Contacts in," she ordered, placing her own quickly back in her eyes. She took one last breath of air, and dove beneath the rising water. Her nose tried to breathe, but she refused to let it, instead focusing on the gills at the base of her neck. Her lungs began to burn again until the water found its way into her gills and she gulped in the life-giving liquid.

She began shaking the Professor again, but he remained limp and unresponsive. She pushed water through his gills, floating him back and forth, for another half an hour before Charlie finally put a hand on her shoulder. "He's gone," he insisted.

Kim's shoulder's shook as she backed away from the lifeless scientist. Her skin burned as she glanced at the others. "Life can no longer exist on land," she announced, trying to regain her composure and sound like the Commander she was supposed to be. "Gentlemen, the world has ended, and we, the city in the Trench, are the only humans left."

# AUSTIN
### By Derek Rutherford

"I've been waiting for you," Frederick Gordon said.
"Well, not *you* in particular. Someone like you." He
was seventy-two years old. His hair was white but
there was plenty of it. In fact at the back it was
almost collar length. He had a neat moustache. He
wore a tweed jacket and brown corduroy trousers. A
woolen tie was neatly knotted at his collar. He
looked every inch the English country gent. And he
had done something so terrible that they had sent
Casey to kill him.

"Would you like a cup of tea?" Gordon
asked.

For a moment Casey stared at him silently,
trying to figure the old man out. What was he still
doing here? If I had been expecting someone like
me, Casey thought, I would have hit the road? Sure
we'd find him wherever he went - it's impossible to
disappear nowadays - but did *he* know that?

"Or sherry," Gordon said, walking over to a long oak sideboard and picking up a decanter. "Maybe you'd rather have sherry?"

He had a family. A daughter, forty-one years old, married with two little girls. They lived in Worthing. Casey had the address. A son, too. Forty-five, single, and living in Aberdeen. Again, Casey had the address. He was a diver. The son, not Frederick. Aberdeen or Worthing? Opposite ends of the country. At least he would have been giving himself a fighting chance. Not like this: a cottage miles from anywhere, not even any neighbours.

"You can't work me out, can you?" Gordon said and laughed. "You think I'm a fool for staying here if I knew you were coming."

Casey said nothing.

Gordon put the decanter down. "Oh for goodness sake, relax man! Let me put the kettle on and then we'll talk about this."

"There's nothing to talk about."

Gordon smiled. He smiled without opening his mouth and he nodded at the same time. It was a smile that said 'Don't worry, young man, I'll explain it all in good time.' He went into the kitchen and Casey heard him filling the kettle.

It was a mistake to get involved. That had been drummed into Casey a thousand times. Get in, do the job, get out. The less you knew about them the better. It was hard enough knowing that he had two pretty little grand-daughters who both had white hair like their grand-dad.

It had to look like an accident. That made it more difficult. You have to kill a stranger, it's simple. So long as no-one sees the two of you together then you're a home and dry. Two bullets are all you need. It takes less than thirty seconds. When, for whatever reason, they want it to look like an accident it's a little more difficult. You have to set things up with a little more care. Casey didn't know why this one had to look like an accident. Orders were orders.

"Milk and sugar?" Gordon asked from the kitchen.

The moment Casey had walked into his cottage he knew how he was going to kill Frederick Gordon. Standing at the front door looking right up those narrow and uneven stairs. It would be so easy for an old man to slip and fall and break his neck down such stairs.

"I assume you know why you're here?" Gordon called from the kitchen. Casey found it hard to believe how cheerful Gordon sounded. He spoke as though Casey was a long lost friend rather than a killer. Gordon appeared in the doorway. "Silly question. Of course you know why you're here. But - and I've always wondered this - do they tell you *why*?" He was straightening his tie as he spoke, making sure it was tight up against his collar.

Casey walked further into the room. Until that moment he'd been standing just inside the front door. It was a small cottage, the type where the front door opens into the living room. The type with thick stone walls. He picked up a photograph from the mantelpiece. The grand-daughters.

"Pretty girls," Casey said, trying to provoke a reaction. He wanted Gordon to be scared. Not because he was cruel but because then he'd be in control. This total disregard for one's impending doom was a little disconcerting.

"Aren't they just?" he said. "Martha and Louise."

"I know," Casey said, and put the photograph back down.

For a moment there was a flicker of concern on Gordon's face when he realized Casey knew the girls' names.

There was a click from the kitchen. "Kettle's boiled," Gordon said quickly. "I'll make the tea." He went back into the kitchen. "Milk and sugar?" he asked again.

He came back in carrying a plastic tray with a china teapot and two china cups and saucers on it. There was a bowl of sugar, a carton of semi-skimmed milk, and an unopened packet of chocolate digestives on the tray. He put the tray down on a small round table and sat down in the armchair alongside it.

"Help yourself." He pointed to the milk and sugar. "You never answered."

"Probably best to let it brew," Casey said. He had no intention of drinking Gordon's tea or eating his biscuits.

Gordon nodded. "Of course. Please sit down."

"I'm okay." Casey stood with his back to the fireplace. It was July. There was no fire in the hearth, just a selection of yellow, brown and red dried flowers arranged in an old copper kettle.

Gordon started fiddling with his tie again.

"You're taking this remarkably well," Casey said.

"Oh, I wouldn't be so sure. If you could see my insides..." He lifted the lid of the teapot and peered inside. Satisfied at what he saw, he poured a tiny drop of milk into a cup and then filled it with tea. He looked up at Casey, eyebrows raised. Casey shook his head. Gordon nodded. He understood that Casey wouldn't be drinking his tea. Gordon put the teapot down and picked up the cup and saucer. His hand shook only very slightly. Under the circumstances Casey found that staggering.

"I'm seventy-two," Gordon said, as if that explained everything. He sipped his tea, then added, "I've also had a lot of time to prepare."

He reached forwards, put the cup and saucer down, and picked up the biscuits. "Digestive? They're unopened."

Casey smiled and shook his head again. Gordon smiled back. Casey cursed himself. It wasn't good to build up even the tiniest relationship.

"Please," he said, "my question of a few minutes ago: do you know *why* you're here? Do you know what it is I've done? Please, I'd really like to know."

"I'm a professional," Casey said. "I get given orders and I carry them out."

"Orders," Gordon said, and shook his head. "Terrible things. Do you not wonder? Do you not look at an old man such as myself and wonder why?"

"I don't think about it," Casey said.

"Oh, but I'm sure you do. Nobody can do what you do and not think about it." Casey went to speak but Gordon raised a hand to stop him and Casey found his jaw snapping shut. "It's not relevant, anyway," Gordon said. "I don't want to sit here arguing about such a mundane thing as whether a soldier should blindly follow his orders -"

"I'm not a soldier."

"Whatever. It doesn't matter anyway. What does matter... what matters to me is that you know why you're here. Would you grant me that much?"

Casey shrugged.

Gordon put down the packet of biscuits, still unopened, and picked up his tea again. He took a sip. His hands had stopped shaking. "Sit down, please."

"I'm all right where I am."

"You know I've had two visits from your people," Gordon said. "I expected them to come a lot sooner than they did. Oh, I suppose these things take a lot longer to filter through the system than one imagines."

"What things would that be?"

"My story. That's why you're here. Because of an old man's story. Oh I signed all of the paper work - the official secrets act, the unofficial secrets act, goodness knows what - and promised not to tell. But when you get to my age you get a lot of time to ponder on things. Some things simply have to be told. They weigh too heavily on your mind if you try and keep them to yourself."

"What were you?" Casey asked, genuinely interested. He, too, had signed similar declarations.

"An English teacher."

"An English teacher?"

"Yes. Please, sit down, and I'll tell you my story."

Casey sat down.

***

"It happened in Nineteen Seventy Four. We - and I say 'we' generically - I wasn't really involved until later - were tracking something from way out. Many times we'd done the same thing, but this time...this time it came all the way. It crashed. Salisbury Plain, would you believe? Terribly good luck. But that wasn't all. Oh, that was amazing enough. But it didn't end there.

"There was a huge hoo-ha over the crash. Internally - not publicly - only a few knew the full story. Those that did know were asking themselves what was the right thing to do? Should we show the world what we had? Or should we keep it quiet and have a good look at it ourselves before making any decisions? The military were very keen on keeping it quiet, of course."

Gordon looked Casey straight in the eyes, his gaze unwavering. "Tell me, what would you have done? Would you have announced that something from another world had crashed into ours and had survived?"

Before Casey had chance to assimilate what Gordon was saying, let alone formulate an answer, Gordon was moving on, talking fast, as if he was scared he might not have enough time to finish his story.

"Well, the military got their way and what we did was to hide this thing away from everyone and nurse it back to health. It was only much *much* later that we wondered what the hell to do with it."

Gordon sipped his tea and looked at Casey over the edge of his cup as if waiting for a reaction. "You're trying to tell me that we had something from another planet?" Casey asked.

Gordon nodded.

"It started off excitingly enough. Here was an *alien*, for goodness sake! There was blood to be tested and cells to analyze. There were strange fibers to examine and fragments of metal to get excited about. There was an odd pear-shaped head for electrodes to be taped to. There were seven orifices to be probed. For months our unit buzzed with excitement and passion. But, of course, such levels of intensity couldn't be maintained and pretty soon it was business as usual to have an alien locked up in the cells below ground. Little by little, as the secrets of its flesh and of its clothes and of its ship were revealed many of those - and there were probably only a dozen of us - who knew of the alien's existence stopped visiting on a daily basis. Sometimes some of them didn't visit for a week or more.

"For me, though, it was different. I was appended to the creature full time. I had a specific job to do. I had to teach it English."

He paused, sipped his tea again, and looked at Casey, his eyebrows raised as if to say 'don't you find that just amazing?' Casey said nothing. He realized he had made a mistake. By now he should have had the job done and been a mile down the road.

"Initially what I did was to keep my distance," Gordon went on. "I didn't have to imagine the terror that this poor creature was going through, I could see it in its many eyes every time a human being went near it. And I knew that sooner or later I was going to have to build up a working relationship with it, so the last thing I wanted was to be associated with this terror. Something else I did: we all wore white laboratory coats (for no reason other than we had always worn white laboratory coats and we could get them for nothing from the stores) and, when dealing with the alien (to start with, at least) rubber gloves and face masks. For the first two or three weeks the appearance of a white coat meant that the alien was about to be injected, penetrated, cut, drained, or scraped. It got so that it couldn't see a white coated figure without curling up into a ball in the corner of the room crying with fear or racing around the cell snarling and lashing out with its claws. So I took to wearing black to disassociate myself from this terror. Also, I never touched it. Not for months, at least.

"It took a long time to get the creature - whom we had christened Austin on account of the crash that had brought it to us was remarkably similar to the crash on the opening credits of the Six Million Dollar Man (or so I was told) - to accept me. For days and days I simply sat in the cell letting him (later we ascertained from Austin himself that he was indeed a male - our chaps not being able to figure it out from their tests) get used to me. Eventually I persuaded him to sit at a table opposite me. I taught him my name. I taught him the names of everything in the cell. His memory, once he cottoned on to what I was doing, was remarkable. He never forgot anything. By the eleventh month of his captivity Austin was recognizing and producing simple sentences. Month twelve, and you could hold a conversation - albcit slowly - with him. All of this work was observed and taped and I knew the boffins were itching to interrogate the alien. I put them off as long as I was able. I had him reading simple books by month fourteen. Writing after a fashion, too. Midway through the creature's second year on earth he suddenly discovered the secrets of our language. Almost overnight he began to talk and listen and understand as if he'd been here all his life. He recounted stories of families and friends, of his home all those millions of miles away, of his loneliness. Could we not help him? he asked. What were we going to do with him? He knew from his flight how big our world was - why was he not allowed out from these few rooms? I was not allowed to answer such questions. I *couldn't* answer such questions. Then, almost as quickly as full understanding of the language had come to him, my place opposite him was taken by the scientists. I had never been told what his flesh and the metal of his ship had revealed to them but whatever it was it would be nothing compared to the secrets within his mind.

"Despite being moved on to a new project I endeavored to keep in touch. Whenever I could I visited Austin, though often I was restricted to looking at him through one of the two way mirrors through which his every move was observed. When I did manage to speak to him he told me how he had missed me, that the others weren't so kind, that all they did was question him, question him, question him. At least with me he had learned things too. My teaching had been a two-way process. How can you explain who you are without talking about your family? How can you explain where you are without talking about your home? I was reminded again about how great his memory was. There wasn't one thing that we had spoken about during our many months together that he had forgotten.

"'You play chess?' he asked me once. His voice was guttural and thick, almost liquid in places. Part of the process I had used to crush the barriers between us was to try and learn some of his language (someone else had the job officially) and I found the words were next to impossible to pronounce.

"I nodded. He had been given a trunk full of books to read. One of them was a compendium of great chess games. He had fathomed out the moves by studying the games. I promised I would get hold of a board and we would have a game next time I visited (this I did, and he beat me nine games to nil).

"My job, however, was done. The creature could speak English."

Gordon looked across at Casey, "You don't believe a word I'm saying, do you?"

It's a good story," Casey said.

"It's more than that," he said. "It's the truth. It's why you're here."

"Who else have you been telling this story to?" Casey asked.

"Anyone who sits still long enough," Gordon said. "I wrote to some newspapers, too."

Casey nodded. "Somebody asked you to stop."

"Twice."

"So why keep doing it?"

"You haven't heard the end yet."

"There's more?"

"Oh yes."

"Go on."

"The question often haunted me in those days of the late seventies: not whether we had been right to keep Austin a secret in the first place, but what should we be doing with him now? What was the right way to proceed? We had learnt all we could from Austin. We did not have the technology to send him home. He did not have the knowledge to help us create that technology. We couldn't just let him go - he would have sent the first person who saw him screaming up a tree. So what could we do? If he had been a spy seeking asylum we would have bled him dry (as we had Austin), taught him a little English (as we had Austin) and given him a new identity and a cottage in Wales. But you couldn't do that to a three feet high alien with scarlet skin and eight claws. And so we did nothing. His cell was made as comfortable as possible and there he stayed.

"And that was something that I thought about almost every day.

"Imagine this… sorry, I don't think I caught your name. How rude of me."

"Casey." The word came out before he could stop himself. It was poor discipline, but in the grand scheme of things it was irrelevant.

"Imagine this, Casey: if you'd have been found guilty of murder in nineteen seventy-four the chances are that you'd have been out by nineteen eighty-six. That's what I was thinking when I visited Austin in July of that year. July of 'eighty-six. We'd had him twelve years by then. As usual he was pleased to see me. We played some cribbage, talked about the World Cup, he taught me some Bulgarian swear words he'd picked up whilst whiling away the time reading European papers and magazines. But he was no longer his old self. The years of confinement were wearing his spirit away. His perfect memory meant that time never dulled the pain he felt at missing his home and his loved ones. Not being able to live on his own world, he said, wouldn't have been so bad if he could be free on ours. But the option wasn't available. Nevertheless, that wasn't the worst thing. On that visit I was struck by something that I had already noticed but had refused to accept, something that ultimately brings you here today.

"I was struck by the fact that Austin wasn't getting any older."

The old man paused. Casey guessed he always paused at this point in his tale. Gordon wanted to let the full enormity of what he was saying sink in.

"I don't mean he was ageing *slowly*. I mean he wasn't ageing *at all*!" He paused again, then: "That was in 'eighty-six. I saw him again three years later. He was still the same! Exactly the same."

Gordon leant forwards in his chair now. He had forgotten, Casey was sure, why he was here. The story was everything. "Don't you understand? We have had a creature locked up for thirty-five years! Are we going to keep it forever?"

He leant back in his chair, then leant forwards again and picked his tea up, but his hand was shaking so much he had to put it back down. Casey found it incredible: his - the assassin's - presence had caused just the merest tremble, the story had left Gordon unable to hold a cup. Gordon mouthed the word *Austin* to himself. His eyes were glistening.

He sat quietly for a moment and then asked: "Would you excuse me for a moment?"

"Sure."

Casey watched Gordon climb those narrow and uneven stairs in the corner of the room and heard a door close at the top.

It could all be bullshit, of course, Casey told himself as he climbed the stairs as quietly as a cat. An old man's imagination. But *something* had brought him here and knowing the Organization it could quite easily be something as strange as this.

He could hear Gordon in the bathroom. There was a tap running. Gordon coughed. A guttural cough, almost liquid. Later, Casey realized he should have paid more attention to that.

Casey looked down the stairs. It would be a hard fall.

And then he found himself wondering if there really was a creature from many millions of miles away incarcerated in a cell somewhere. A creature who, for all anyone knew, might live forever. A creature with a perfect memory pining for his home and family. If such a creature did exist what would happen to it? Then he started to wonder exactly *where* this creature was being held and if it mightn't be possible to check it out.

The old man coughed again and Casey cursed Gordon for planting such seeds in his mind. He should never have listened to the man's story.

Then Gordon opened the door and Casey realized how he'd been fooled. The old man's story was true, at least to a point. In the split second he had to consider these things he realized that he hadn't been sent here because the old man had been telling his story to newspapers. Jesus, he wouldn't dare tell anyone about *this!* There *was* a creature. But it was no longer locked away in a cell.

A moment later, as far as Casey was concerned, such things didn't matter anymore.

# THE LAST SOLDIER
## By John J. Rust

*Today is the day the Ka'yean die.*

The thought sent a shudder through Hn'nen's long, green, stick-like body. He lowered his conical head, staring at his reflection in the small pond next to him. His dark, bulging eyes swept over his four thin legs and four arms. A gurgle escaped his throat. Only five years ago, the Ka'yean had numbered seven billion.

How could he be the last one?

Would it not be more fitting for the last one to be an intellectual, a music maker, an educator? Someone who could perhaps leave the story of his race in a data node for some other race to find in the future, so the Ka'yean would not be forgotten?

Instead, he was all that remained of his race. A common soldier. Not even a squad leader. Just some drone whose only purpose was to pull a trigger and show deference to his leaders.

*How is it I am the last Ka'yean?* Hn'nen had no idea how many rotation cycles he asked himself that question. Another question also plagued his mind.

What should he do about it?

Hide, of course. He couldn't let the enemy get hold of him. He'd seen enough reports on what happened to those taken prisoner. He shuddered thinking of those death camps. The methods they used . . . he couldn't believe an advanced civilization could treat sentient beings that way.

No, he couldn't let himself be captured. He wouldn't. Better to die quickly than endure whatever agony the enemy wished to inflict on him. And being the last Ka'yean, those beasts would likely extend his suffering as long as possible.

Hn'nen looked over the weapons in front of him. This is how he would die. Like a true soldier.

A couple squeals burst from his mouth. He didn't want to die. He'd only just entered his adulthood period. There was so much more life ahead of him.

*I could still hide. I can always live off roots and soil.* Plus the Trn'iey continental mass was vast, and contained numerous mountains and deserts. He could hide there for the rest of his natural life without the enemy finding him.

*And do what?*

*Not die.*

The Ka'yean race would live on through him, for a while anyway. That had to be preferable this suicide mission he had planned. Dying like a soldier. Striking one final blow in the name of his soon-to-be-extinct race. What purpose would that serve? Who would celebrate his sacrifice? Would the enemy remember it for many solar cycles to come, or would they treat it as a mere annoyance and forget about it after a single rotation cycle?

Living would be a form of resistance, would it not? The enemy probably thought they had eliminated all Ka'yean. He could prove them wrong for many solar cycles. He could spew waste in their collective pale faces by simply surviving.

*Is that enough, though?*

An old saying crept into his mind, one by the great intellectual Klk'res. *"There is much difference between living and merely existing."*

What would his existence be like if he decided not to go through with his plan? Living in caves, eating and sleeping, perhaps torturing himself with memories of what life was like before the invasion.

Worst of all, he would be alone. How many solar cycles could he go without any companionship before he went insane?

Another thought entered his mind. If he lived out the rest of his life in a cave, wouldn't that mean the enemy had beaten him?

*The enemy has beaten me. They've beaten my entire race.*

Hn'nen huffed at that thought. No, they haven't beaten the entire Ka'yean. He still lived. He could still fight.

One last fight.

All his muscles tensed, trying to fight off the fearful shudders that threatened to overwhelm him. He drew long, controlled breaths as he picked up his weapons and equipment, trying to focus his mind on one thing.

The mission.

He skittered over the rocks and shrubs until he came to a rise. His mouth went dry when he beheld the sight before him.

A dozen silver domes of various sizes sat at the bottom of the barren valley, surrounded by a laser fence. Weapons towers rose from the ground, bristling with gun tubes and rockets.

In the middle of the compound, a pole protruded from the ground. Hn'nen buzzed in fury as he set his eyes on the blood red flag with that black, twisted symbol in the center. He never imagined he could hate a colored piece of cloth so much.

*It's time.*

Hn'nen tapped the control band on his wrist. A dozen small, spheroid objects rose from his supply pack and hurtled toward the enemy compound. With another click of his control band his eye implants called up a digital display of the target and measured the progress of the combat drones. The two assigned to jamming duties had already shut down the enemy sensor network and laser fence. The enemy war computers, however, would counter those effects shortly.

But they would be too late.

Joy surged through Hn'nen as miniature white suns detonated throughout the compound. The weapons towers and huge chunks of the domes vanished as the plasma demolition drones did their work.

The surveillance drones beamed images to his eye implants of numerous bipedal beings emerging from the wrecked domes. Some wore battle armor, some wore simple black coverings. Many were covered in red blood or had missing appendages. The ones with their heads uncovered all had fair hair.

Hn'nen clutched personal assault weapons in each of his four hands. All four stubby weapons were loaded with nano-projectiles, designed to eat through battle armor, and the flesh behind it.

Several bipedal soldiers charged out of the smoking compound, headed in his direction. He tried to accept his fate, but couldn't. Hn'nen did not want to die. Unfortunately, he did not have much to live for.

A flicker of anger rose within him. Not anger at the enemy, but anger at a collection of beings that existed in the very distant past. He thought back to the captured historical records of the enemy, ones that spoke of a great war hundreds of solar cycles ago on their native world of Earth. What if this collective known as "The Allies" had defeated these bipedals who worshipped the screaming lunatic with that little growth of hair under his nose? The universe could have been spared so much evil and suffering.

But that did not happen. And his race paid the price for it.

Hn'nen's eyes swept over the valley. Nearly a hundred enemy soldiers swarmed toward him.

A high-pitched shriek exploded from his mouth. He charged at the bipedals, all four guns firing away. A blurry white substance spread over several soldiers, devouring them.

A barrage of enemy lasers streaked across the valley.

Hn'nen took a hit, then another. Another. Another.

Pain burned through his body. He wanted to shriek. Instead he kept his fingers down on all four triggers, hurling death at the enemy. A feeling flared inside him, one he never anticipated for this final mission.

Happiness.

Between his nano-projectiles and his plasma demolitions, he must have killed hundreds of enemy soldiers. But he thought about the survivors more. Some would certainly talk about what one lone Ka'yean did. They would tell other bipedals, who would probably tell their offspring, who might tell their offspring, and so on and so forth.

Even as the life faded from his body, Hn'nen took comfort in the fact that, in some way, the Ka'yean would live forever.

# WHAT IF ROSE WAS RIGHT
## *By Grace Gannon Rudolph*

Lightning flickered inside the dark roiling cloud hovering over the Golden Ladder Nursing Home.

Earlier that night, before her nurse's aide helped Rose into bed, Rose had watched the evening news. Rose, ninety-one, was a news addict. She was alert and oriented but tormented by intractable pain.

"That's just foolish," the aide said, gently readjusting Rose's pillow and putting up the side-rails.

"What's foolish?" Rose asked.

"'Reported sightings of a space ship'. Humph."

"Why is it foolish?" Rose asked.

"Near here? Nothing happens near here."

"Maybe it's in that cloud." Rose pointed to the thick cloud hiding the full moon outside her window.

"That's just heat lightning."

The aide began to pull the drapes across the window but stopped when Rose said, "No, I want to look out."

"Looking for space ships?" The aide smiled as she paused in the doorway. "You want the light on or off?"

"Off."

The soft hum of voices at the nurse's station was comforting but Rose was in for another sleepless night. She turned her head on the pillow and faced the window. Suddenly the trees outside bowed towards the earth, as though crushed by and unseen hand.

Lois, the evening nurse knocked gently on the door before slipping into the darkened room. "Rose, are you awake?" Rose turned her head. "I just wanted to say goodnight." Lois slipped the strap of her pocketbook higher on her shoulder.

"Do you have a minute?"

Lois glanced at her watch and sat down on the chair next to Rose's bed. "Not long. I'm working at the hospital after I leave here."

"The maternity ward again?"

Lois nodded.

"There's a full moon. There'll be a lot of babies."

"I like to keep busy. When you're fifty-five and single and have a mortgage to pay -"

"You know what I think," Rose interrupted, "I think babies can't speak until they forget their former lives, where they lived, what they saw."

"Rose," Lois chuckled.

"No, I mean it." She turned back to the window. "You know what else I think?" Lois shook her head. "It isn't what I *think*, it's what I *know*."

"I'll bet you know a lot of things," Lois smiled.

"See that cloud?" Lois looked out the window. "It's not a cloud," Rose whispered into the darkness. "A little while ago a door inside that cloud opened and a golden ladder came out."

Lois took Rose's hand. "Honey," she said, "this is the Golden Ladder Nursing Home." She bit her lower lip and frowned.

"I know that," Rose pulled her hand away. "But I know what I saw. Someone, I couldn't make them out, came down the ladder and reached through the window. Their arm was long and thin and their fingers were beautiful. I knew if I took that hand I would have followed them up the ladder and never looked back."

Lois decided to play along; to meet Rose where she was. "And then what?"

Rose shrugged. "I don't know." They sat in silence for a moment until Rose said, "If I find out do you want me to let you know?"

"Sure," Lois stood up. Before she left she needed to alert the nurse on duty that Rose's change in mental status could be the beginning of an infection and she needed to be monitored.

"Do you have to go?"

Lois nodded.

At the doorway she turned back when Rose said softly, "If I'm not here when you get back don't worry. I'll make sure to give you a sign."

In the silence and shadows of the near empty parking lot Lois looked up at the starless sky. The cloud *did* seem to hover in place.

By the time she reached the hospital, the maternity ward was a hive of activity and Lois forgot about the cloud.

Abby Eddelman, a first time mother in the room across from the nursing station, was the first name on Lois' assignment sheet. Before going in to take the young woman's vital signs Lois called the nursing home. "How's Rose?" she asked.

"Oh, Lois, I'm so sorry. She passed away right after you left."

Lois replaced the receiver and buried her face in her hands for a moment, then stood up and crossed the hall to Abby Eddelman's room.

Abby, her damp hair pulled back in a pony tail, was cuddling her baby in the crook of her arm. Her husband James sat on the edge of the bed holding the baby's tiny fist in his hand and studying the fragile fingers. His tie was undone and his shirt was rumpled.

"Congratulations," Lois said as she folded the blood pressure cuff around Abby's arm. "What's the baby's name?"

"We didn't know if it was going to be a boy or a girl so we haven't picked out a name," James said.

The young couple looked at each other for a moment and then, together, said, "Rose," and began to laugh. "Where did *that* come from," James said.

"Is that your mother's name?" Lois asked.

They shook their heads. "We don't have anybody in the family with that name," Abby said, running her finger down the side of the baby's cheek, "until now. So, Rose, how do you like your name?"

The baby turned its head towards Lois. "Look," James grinned, "Rose smiled."

"Honey, that's just gas," Abby said.

Lois reached down and cupped the baby's head in the palm of her hand. "Hello Rose," she whispered. "Welcome back."

# HERD MENTALITY
### By Paul A. Freeman

Doctor Angus, the veterinarian, made an incision around the top of the dead herd animal's skull. He handed the scalpel back to Daisy, his assistant. "Saw!" he barked.

The rotating blade of the surgical saw cut deep enough to separate a cap of skin and bone from the rest of the creature's skull. Doctor Angus worked the cap loose and tugged. It came away, exposing the herd animal's degenerated brain.

"What were the animal's symptoms?" Doctor Angus asked.

Daisy checked her notes. "There was general disorientation, and an inability to stand unaided. This was followed by deterioration of brain functions and death."

Later, in the histology lab, Doctor Angus took tissue samples from the dead animal's brain and prepared a series of slides. Daisy stained the slides with iodine, and the veterinarian examined them under a microscope.

"The brain cortex is compromised," said Doctor Angus. "It's full of holes. It looks almost like a sponge."

"Spongiform encephalopathy?" asked Daisy.

Doctor Angus nodded, and in that parallel universe where cattle were the dominant species, the veterinarian prayed that no bovine variant of 'Mad Human Disease' would develop. After all, human burgers were his and Daisy's favorite fast food.

# A SPLASH OF ORANGE
## *By Harper Hull*

Kosmonauts Helger and Farmer took their first steps on the surface of Venus. In their bright tangerine spacesuits and helmets they stood out immediately against the harsh, muted grain landscape; a painter's wet brush dripping on an old unused canvas. Lightning crashed above them and a rapid wind whipped dust into funnels and eddies that jumped and jigged across the ground like tiny tornados. Farmer slowly walked around the rocket ship to the transport bay and attempted to unseal the main doors. They made a stuttering whooshing sound but wouldn't open.

"James, this thing isn't opening up" he said into his helmet communicator.

Helger joined Farmer at the bay doors and tried the locking mechanism himself.

"I know I overrode the internal lock, must be a mechanical failure."

Farmer made an exaggerated head turn in his large helmet and looked at Helger.

"Good start, huh, pal? Can't even get the goddam Goblin out. Are we supposed to walk to Terra Magellan from here?"

"Give me a minute," replied Helger, "let me see if I can work it out."

Farmer wandered back around to the front of the rocket and surveyed the land. Dust was blowing towards them predominantly from the low hills ahead. These were the hills of the planet of love(technically they were a mass of impact craters) that they needed to cross to get to the Magellan base which was situated in a small valley almost right in the middle of this range, isolated yet protected. Without their vehicle it would be a long hike, through a dark evening of lightning and thunder, and something no kosmonaut had attempted before. The sooner they got a dock built at Magellan the better, Farmer thought. The light on Venus was dim, at least here where they were, due in part to the huge radiation deflectors that were hanging in the sky miles above them. Massive white shields that protected Venus from the Sun's energy, there were crews of WASA engineers and scientists manning each and every deflector, living in sizeable space hubs behind the shields that were dwarfed by the sheer scope of the protective structures. The nickname in the Agency for these workers was *bouncers*. Farmer kind of wished he was a bouncer right now, comfortably quartered and high enough above Venus and the electrical storm to not care. Drinking hot coffee, eating a sandwich, sitting down on soft chairs wearing comfortable clothing. Breathing without the aid of equipment, yeah, that sounded good. The streaking arrows of energy far above kept illuminating the gargantuan white walls for a split second at a time; it looked ominous from down on the planet's surface, and it was hard to believe that man, with all his imperfections and hang-ups, had created them. Being on Venus itself was freaking Farmer out a little, and he wasn't sure why. No-one was more highly trained for this scenario than himself and Helger. He checked his suit readings and everything was fine. Just fine. Still, the very alien sensory tapestry of color, sound and views was disconcerting to say the least. He shivered inside his suit.

"Hey Mike…"

Helger's voice reverberated inside Farmer's helmet.

"…this thing is screwed."

"We walking?"

"Yeah…"

"How long do you think?"

"Long enough, I'm going to fill a couple of suitbags with supplies and we should get going."

"Roger that. Oh, Jim, make sure the ship coms are on remote, and let Earth Base know what's happened."

"Of course man, of course. Back in a few. Stay low."

It took the two kosmonauts almost three hours to reach the top of the first flat hill, even though it had seemed a lot closer from the vantage point of the rocket ship. Helger was operating the tracker device and keeping them going in the right direction; Farmer was looking around and taking occasional readings on his *ultrometer* – temperature, radiation, carbon dioxide levels, moisture, wind speed, light. They were the first men to set foot on Venus since the Terraformers at Magellan had arrived twenty something years ago, and WASA Earth Base wanted any information they could gather, a new perspective from fresh eyes and minds. The working colony at Magellan had been out of contact for a while – exactly how long, no-one had told Helger and Farmer – and their mission here was to ensure everybody was all right, and help fix any damaged communications equipment. Both men carried weapons, as was standard practice in the Kosmonaut Corp since the Europa incident; each had an *SM-5 Recon Rifle* attached to their upper right leg. The SM-5, aka The Stabber, was a short, lightweight weapon that packed a powerful punch at short range. It also utilized an ultra strong 10-inch armor-piercing bayonet, a new addition in recent years harking back to the ancient wars of man when killing was done face to face. The Kosmonaut Corp never knew what they'd be coming in contact with, what kind of weaponry would be effective; a blade was considered universally applicable and wouldn't fail like an electric or gas powered weapon could. Man had not encountered any kind of Venusian life-form to date, although some years ago Magellan had sent Earth images of what could have been massive abstract sculptures found far off in the Northern Plains. The general consensus amongst the boffins back home had been that it was a coincidental effect caused by geology, and that had been that.

Helger stopped at the crest of the impact crater and looked around, checked the tracker, looked around again. Thunder boomed way above him.

"If we had the Goblin I'd say go straight down and round the inner bowl of this thing, but on foot, let's skirt the edge and go around that way." He glanced down and attached the tracker back on his belt.

Farmer was about to reply when he spotted a colorful flash on the other side of the crater, right at the lip.

"Jim, look, 1 o'clock."

Helger looked up and caught a glimpse of orange disappearing out of view.

"The Hell is that?" he asked.

"It looked like people wearing our bio-rads...they don't have any Corp at Magellan do they?"

"Not that I know of," said Helger, shaking his head slowly, "just the 'formers and colonials...they wouldn't have any BR suits. They all use the deep pressure numbers here now." "Could another ship have landed? Nah, we'd know about it." Farmer squinted, confused. "Get on the com and ask Base if they have any idea what's going on up here."

Helger accessed his Base com via the ship's relay and started reciting his security code. Farmer wondered if the incessant lightning was playing tricks on them across the yellow crater. He kept his eyes fixed on the point where the strangers had disappeared from view, but they didn't return.

They were unable to make contact with Base, for some reason the rocket ship relay was offline despite Helger having set it up before they took off on their trek. Farmer felt like they were well and truly Jonah'd already - the inaccessible Goblin, the unidentified figures and now no external com.

Skirting around the rim of the huge crater Helger changed his com setting to pick up any local transmissions, hoping to get some kind of signal from Terra Magellan. The two men moved as fast as they could towards the opposite side of the crater lip, Farmer instinctively placing his gloved right hand on the butt of his Stabber. As they cleared the outer crest and were able to see what lay beyond the first crater, they both stopped dead, catching their breath and looking out ahead of them. Craters. Nothing but large craters as far as they could see. A wash of pale mustard and flax sand lit up by the white strobes of lightning.

"Where did they go?" asked Helger, pulling a scope from his belt and putting it up to his helmet visor. "I don't see…wait!" Helger stiffened and his whole body froze, statuesque in posture.

Farmer followed Helger's gaze and immediately saw them himself. Off to the left, two figures were just below the lip of one of the massive craters. Farmer took the scope from Helger and zoomed in on the figures quickly, before they dropped out of sight again. It certainly looked like a pair of kosmonauts, they wore the distinct orange bio-rad suits and Farmer could even make out

Stabbers slung at their hips, despite the dust swirling and roping around their bodies. As the unknown pair were about to fall out of view, they stopped moving and looked back. One of them pointed towards Helger and Farmer, and then both strangers disappeared, fast, over the crater's lip. They were gone like stones thrown off a cliff into an endless ocean.

Without having to consult, Helger and Farmer both took off as quickly as their spacesuits and boots would allow. No skirting carefully around the massively wide crater this time, they launched themselves into the ankle-deep dusty shallows and headed left, straight towards where the two strangers had just disappeared. With long, loping, ungainly strides the two kosmonauts left a yellow cloud trail in their wake which was picked up and swirled by the constant wind eddying down into the crater. With one eye on the distant perimeter and one on the rocky ground, this was reckless abandon, and both men knew it. They could turn an ankle or worse very easily going at this pace in such rough terrain. This was against everything they had been taught in training. Control was paramount; control was your emotional God. Neither man cared, something was very, very wrong about this situation and they needed to get answers immediately. With the already dark sky turning a deep shade of indigo above them, Farmer was first to the far side and began scrambling up the loose, shingle scattered slope, dead daffodil colored dust clouding up around his helmet and obscuring his already limited view. He heard Helger clawing the gravel right behind him, and it didn't take long for both men to reach the brow, huffing and puffing at the exertion and extra drain on their oxygen supplies. Without pausing for breath or taking a second to wipe down their filthy visors, both men continued over the crest and straight down the loose slope into the next basin. Waiting at the bottom with weapons drawn were the two strangers in orange, each down on one knee. Helger and Farmer barely had time to see them, let alone react, as they slid down the scree out of control, trying to backpedal desperately in the puffing pollen ground. Two blasts exploded from the weapons below them, blinding flashes of blue as loud as the thunder in the horribly close Venusian night, and Helger and Farmer were thrown backwards against the loose rocky slope as more lightning whip lashed in the Heavens. The last thing they saw was the dark sky swirling above them, and then their bodies slid down into the crater, motionless.

A crackling voice in the dark. Robotic. Emotionless.

*"Leave the planet, you cannot help, repeat, leave here now. You are in danger. To anyone present, please go home. You cannot reach us. We cannot reach you. This is Terra Magellan's emergency broadcast system. We are intact and in control, no aid is needed. Repeat, no aid is needed."*

Farmer blinked his eyes and instinctively threw his hands up to his dusty helmet visor, moving his gloved fingers all over it. It felt intact. He breathed in deeply. No loss of oxygen. Sitting up he looked down his body, checked his arms and legs. No tears, no burns. To his left Helger stirred. Farmer rolled over onto his side and checked out Helger's helmet and suit. Also intact. The crackling voice kept spitting out of Helger's com unit.

*"Please go home. You cannot reach us."*

Lightning zigzagged across the skies and the reception turned to static for a moment. Helger pulled himself up on his elbows and looked at Farmer.

"You OK?"

Farmer nodded slowly.

"Seem to be...what the Hell happened there? You saw the Stabbers go off right? Did they miss us and take off when we...passed out?"

Helger shook his head.

"Maybe they didn't discharge correctly and just concussed us. I dunno. How long were we out?"

Farmer checked his watch.

"I'm not sure what time it was when we got here" he said, puzzled.

*"You cannot help, repeat, leave here now."*

"Who's this guy?" asked Farmer, tapping his com unit.

"Says he's at Magellan. No codes though, could be a trick."

"A trick by who?"

"Whoever tried to kill us here some unknown amount of time ago, who else?"

Helger sighed, got to his feet and pointed back up the ridge they had slid down.

"I'm going to go take a look from up there, see if I can see….well, anything. Something. Whatever."

"I'll come with you," said Farmer, also standing up, "my legs need to stretch out. They don't feel quite there."

*"We are intact."*

"And turn that shit off, yeah?"

Click.

The two kosmonauts pulled themselves back up the steep embankment, both feeling confused and more than a little scared. Farmer played through scenarios quickly in his head. What if the broadcast message was actually coming from Magellan? Why were they trying to turn help away? Were they being coerced into it or was something bad really going on in the enormous circle of impact craters surrounding the colony? Maybe they were really trying to warn them against something that lay ahead. The two intruder kosmonauts, for example.

Up on the ridge it seemed a little lighter, the visibility was slightly better, the dust clouds less dense. The two men ran their eyes across the landscape, first ahead of them towards where Magellan should be, then back where they'd already been, towards the rocket ship. Farmer shouted out "Look!" and pointed, grabbing Helger's arm with his hanging hand. The two impostors in the orange spacesuits were on the opposite ridge, it appeared as if they were looking at them through a scope.

"Down, down!" yelled Helger, grabbing Farmer's shoulder, and they went shooting back down the gravelly slope into the basin, both drawing their weapons on the way. At the flattish bottom Helger drew his rifle and indicated to Farmer that he should do the same.
"This doesn't seem right," said Farmer, quietly.

"Aim at the top of the lip, get a good aim, steady aim, balance yourself," yelled Helger, dropping to a knee and weighting his shooting elbow on it.

"I don't think this is supposed to happen," said Farmer, but he also dropped down to a knee and assumed the shooting stance. "Don't you think this is wrong, James?"

"Shhhh…listen for them coming man, listen. We take them down; we don't mess up like they did. Check your weapon and concentrate."

The sound of boots scrunching on tiny rocks got closer and closer, Helger was whispering obscenities to himself and Farmer was trying to turn a key in his mind, open the lock to what was so wrong about all this. Before he could, the two strange figures came flying over the ridge above them.

"Now!" shouted Helger, and his rifle blasted blue at the exact same time as Farmers.

The strangers' bodies slid down the scree and stopped right in front of the two kosmonauts, both still gripping their rifles, fingers on triggers. Farmer stood up and looked down on his victim. A huge hole had ripped through their spacesuit at the chest, burnt orange material ragged and smoking around a bloody cavity that seemed to go right through the body to the ground beneath. Helger's target was in a similar state, shot just below the neckline. Farmer let his eyes pull away from the horror he had caused and float up to the man's helmet. He couldn't see a face beneath the darkened visor, just a nametag across the top rim. It said *FARMER, J.* He heard Helger shouting with a thick tongue and fat lips, and knew what the nametag on the other helmet said without having to look.

"What do we do now?" spat Helger, "what the Hell do we do now? What *is* this?"

Farmer looked from the dead men to Helger before shooting his eyes up towards the dense sky above. Something tapped a beat in his head. Nothing mattered anymore – the mission, the colony, the whole damn planet – he didn't care.

"I think if we want to, we can just go up there, as far as we desire, as fast or as slow as we like." He dropped his weapon and put his arms down against his sides.

Helger watched as his friend started to drift upwards into the air. He felt a beat sound in his head, too.

"We were never supposed to come here, James!" shouted Farmer from above Helger's head. "Come with me. We're done here!"

Helger threw his rifle to the dust and, to his delight, followed Farmer up into the dark clouds, rising at will, his chest filling with all of space and time. Both of them looked down at the dead bodies and mourned their loss, for a second, before waves of bliss covered them, calmed them. They tasted the entire universe in their mouths, the far depths of space twinkled behind their eyes. Higher and higher they rose, invisible to the humans and their machines manning the radiation deflectors above the planet, until they could see a huge swathe of Venusian landscape dipping and curving beneath them, including the Terra Magellan base. It looked derelict, abandoned, no signs of life; a ramshackle town of yellowed metal without a heartbeat. Neither of them cared or felt surprise, as they unfurled their swirling fingers, pulled off their liquid gloves, released their misty helmets and swam up through the stars into eternity, laughing.

Down on the planet's surface, the Earth colony known as Terra Magellan stood dark and silent, except for a single room where a looped radio broadcast played over and over.

A few miles south-west of the ghost colony lay the bodies of two dead kosmonauts, rapidly becoming buried in grainy, goldenrod dust that ramped up their legs and arms, drifted across their chests and started to cover their helmets, until there was barely a strip of tangerine suit left showing.

# PRECIPITATION AND DEVOTION:
## Memoirs of a Raindrop
### *By Stevie Poppe*

*"Who am I? What am I? Why am I here?"*
  These were several questions I had asked myself when I was first born. Although, 'born' probably wouldn't be the best of expressions to use in this situation, as I'd soon realize that I was actually conceived by a meteorological process of precipitate nature...
  In short, I'm a raindrop. Yeah, I know, I know. Most of you readers out there aren't likely to find any importance or appreciation in that brief period between my creation and my fast approaching downfall. And that's not something I can blame you for either. After all, these things *do* happen on a regular basis. If anyone did actually care, they'd be nothing short of crazy, wouldn't they? Well, doesn't matter anyway, I won't digress any longer and just go ahead with it. I'm gonna tell

you exactly that what I had just mentioned – *the story of my life!*

So yeah. Soon after my creation, I came to realize that my existence was a pretty meaningless one. After all, what am I but one of billions of raindrops that fall down on earth every single day, over and over again? Like many of my brothers and sisters, I left a rather individualistic approach to life and, quite honestly, even existence itself. I started spending all of my time coming up with self-destructive thoughts that left me more and more depressed. Life, death… all of it sounded so meaningless to me.

I specifically remember when I said to myself, "Just wait for the end of it all, okay? Wait for that brief moment where I hit the ground and lose my conscience… Surely the void would be preferable to my pointless and solitary struggle for actual meaning, wouldn't it?"

Believe me when I say that being born just to realize that your end is approaching soon and you'll never reach anything lasting is no fun at all. Hey, like I just said, for a short while there, I was actually preparing myself to accept this cursed faith of mine, and embrace the end of my trivial existence.

"It won't take long now. Soon, it will all be over. *Soon*," I kept whispering to myself back then, holding back my manly tears. Yes. Even raindrops are capable of crying. But these thoughts didn't last very long. "NO!!! I will not accept this foolishness!" I cried out in a sudden outburst of emotions.

I understood; from then, everything made perfect sense. After all, what is a drop of rain compared to a full blown storm? If I worked this out well I could make our unity, our comradeship, one of great importance. I found that after my sudden display of energy, a lot of raindrops around me awoke from their self-centered depression and began to stare at me in great curiosity. That is when I held my life-changing speech.

The feeling... I felt reborn, as if I was a new raindrop. I felt *different*. So I started talking, "My brothers, my sisters... Listen to my words! Listen to what I am about to say now!"

I had to quickly improvise a motivational speech. "Alone, we are worth nothing! You've all experienced this feeling. A feeling of self-pity and worthlessness, as if there is no use in going on! With no way to actually change your destiny..."

I remember taking a second to look around me; looking directly into the sad little puppy eyes of many of my brethren. I found it cute in one way yet disgusting in another. It reminded me of my past self, that selfish little raindrop that I was but a mere few seconds ago. I knew very well I was on to something here.

I was convinced I could give some meaning to their lives, and by that, give meaning to my own. First I had to think of a common goal, though. "A common enemy perhaps? Well, maybe…just maybe this could work out to be something quite interesting," I let out under my breath.

"Look, there is only one way out of this mess, and that is for us to work together! If we do that, we can realize the impossible and go where no raindrop has ever gone before. If we combine our forces, there's nothing we can't reach!"

Then it struck me. That moment, I knew exactly what I was meant to do; my very goal in life. I took a short break before continuing this inspiring little speech of mine, because I was barely able to contain myself anymore. It really felt as if I had transcended all ordinary consciousness and as a result reached something much higher, like a higher state of being or something like that.

"Comrades, how much longer will our kind need to feel this way? How much longer will our natural habitat be destroyed by those puny, pathetic creatures of flesh and bone calling themselves the rulers of the world? The rulers of *our* world? Hahaha, don't make me laugh! Who on earth do they think they are? I tell you now, my friends, the time has come at last… THE TIME WHERE WE CHANGE THIS ALL! We can… Wait no, we WILL take back our natural habitat, that which was supposed to be OURS! NOT. THOSE. FILTHY. LITTLE. HUMANS. NOT. THEM. OURS! MINE! HAHAHA!"

It felt like everything was falling into place. In what were mere seconds for those few human readers still alive, I started a full-blown revolution. Just. Like. *That*. I was looking around me while catching my breath and realized there were so many of us and so little of them. There was seriously no way this couldn't have worked.

My people's eyes were shining so brightly, filled with a never before seen hope. Strapping young lads, all of them ready to execute my every command. In mere moments we'd arrive on earth, but I knew now that none of us would lose our minds. None of us would dissolve into the ground and wither away. No, we would remain. We could do this, we could make this happen.

I finished the rest of my speech shortly before we arrived, "Soon… Men of the sky! Soon we will arrive, and let me tell you now: We will conquer and destroy, and from the burning remains of the human empire we will build ourselves a new world. YES! Everything is clear now! Hahaha. HA! HAH! My fellow partners in revolution, let us do this, shall we? Some of you will fall, but do not worry, it will be for the greater good. And I know for sure that, when the time is right, we will all meet again in heaven. Surely, the world will shiver and shake in fear. YAAAAAAAAY."

The moment of truth arrived shortly after. When we reached earth, we spent a short time planning everything out before finally commencing the revolution. Even the weakest warriors amongst us managed to retain their memories and personality for a long enough period to proceed with the battle, and what a battle it was indeed! Hoh hoh! We poisoned your waters. Destroyed your homes. Tore you appart from their insides. Blinded you with rainbows. There was no end to the madness and carnage. You never saw it coming, and everything went according to plan.

The world is ours now. Mine! We did it, and no one was able to stop us. One cannot really imagine the impact this had left on me, the greatness of it all. Not even I was able to fully grasp it at first, but I did know I liked it. Yes, I sure did like it. And what am I doing now, you ask? Well, I'm just sitting here on my throne; the raindrop who took over the world. Hey, it never felt so good being a raindrop before.

# ABOUT THE AUTHORS

## *Valerie Hodge*

Valerie Hodge is a 20 year old student from Newfoundland who is currently completing a double major in English and Psychology at Memorial University. She has written several novels and books of short stories under the genre of Science Fiction and Fantasy, and has succeeded in various publications of her work.

## *Kelli A. Wilkins*

Kelli Wilkins ([www.KelliWilkins.com](www.KelliWilkins.com)) writes in several genres including sci fi, horror, and romance. Dozens of her sci fi stories were once published in the *Sun*.

## *Marian Powell*

Marian has publications for short science fiction stories in four anthologies.

## Ian Lamberto

Ian currently lives in Buffalo, NY, and spends most of his free time working on finishing a first novel

## Justin R Woolley

Justin Woolley makes things up and sometimes writes them down. He has previously published short stories and has an upcoming graphic novel in the works.

## Dixie Sorensen

Dixie Sorensen wants to teach English. She loves to write.

## John J. Rust

John J. Rust is a native of New Jersey who now resides in Prescott, AZ, where he is a radio sports reporter.

### Grace Gannon Rudolph

Grace Gannon Rudolph, a published writer and a social worker, hopes to find an agent for her collection of short stories.
www.gracegannonrudolph.com

### Paul A. Freeman

Paul A. Freeman lives and works in Abu Dhabi. He is the author of Rumours of Ophir, a crime novel set in Zimbabwe, and a children's book, Kimberly Smith and the Pyramid Game. He has had several short stories published in anthologies, newspapers and magazines.

### Stevie Poppe

Steve is an IT student who currently lives in Belgium.

### Harper Hull

Harper Hull grew up in England and lives in the American South where he pens short stories and works on his debut novel 'A Hanging Rock Fall'

### Derek Rutherford

UK based, Derek has been published in The Horrow Show, Fear, Back Street Heroes, All Hallows, Well Told Tales, Malpractice, Arkham Tales, and Escape Velocity.

### Don Magin

Don Magin has lived in Bon Air, Virginia for 32 years, although he and his wife Margaret will always call upstate New York home.

### Jennifer Caddell

Jennifer has a BA in English and enjoys writing Sci-fi, Urban Fantasies, Poetry, Short Stories, Middle Grade fiction, and Young Adult fiction.